Grateful Hearts

Gail Chianese

Annie's®
AnniesFiction.com

Books in The Inn at Magnolia Harbor series

Library of Congress-in-Publication Data
Grateful Hearts / by Gail Chianese
p. cm.
I. Title
                    2019949985

AnniesFiction.com
(800) 282-6643
The Inn at Magnolia Harbor™
Series Creator: Shari Lohner
Editor: Lorie Jones
Cover Illustrator: Bonnie Leick

10 11 12 13 14 | Printed in China | 9 8 7 6 5 4 3 2 1

1

Eden

Downtown Magnolia Harbor, South Carolina, was everything the online brochure promised: quaint, colorful, and utterly charming with cobblestone streets and pots of red and gold mums overflowing along the sidewalk. And thankfully, it wasn't as quiet as Eden Masterson had feared.

But it was an odd little town. People strolled in and out of shops and waved—actually waved—to others doing the same. A few folks even sat on benches and chatted with each other.

People in Eden's hometown of Atlanta, Georgia, didn't wave at each other or loiter on benches. They were always on the go, hustling from home to the office to the gym to the store and back home again. If they were lucky, they had dinner with their families before dropping into bed to repeat everything the next day. Except for Eden. After scarfing down whatever dinner she'd picked up on the way home, she usually put in several more hours of work.

She sighed and shook her head. Magnolia Harbor was like stepping into Oz. A very Southern Oz. Hopefully, the town came without any wicked witches or flying monkeys. Her doctor would never approve of them.

If Eden had written the brochure for Magnolia Harbor, she would have promised visitors that they'd be swept back to a simpler time, to the land of old oaks and sweet magnolia blossoms, of porch swings and sweet tea.

Just what her doctor had ordered.

Just what her body needed to heal.

Just not what she was used to at all.

Eden continued the short drive out of town until she reached her destination, the Magnolia Harbor Inn. She turned up the long driveway, lined with flowers, oak trees, and Spanish moss. The three-story antebellum mansion was breathtaking. Honestly, she wouldn't have been surprised to see Scarlett O'Hara and Rhett Butler from *Gone with the Wind* step onto the wraparound porch.

Instead, a ball of fur sped around the side of the house and made a beeline for her car. Then, to Eden's surprise, the dog sat quietly with his tail wagging, as if waiting for Eden to exit her vehicle. As greeting parties went, she couldn't have been more pleased.

Her phone binged, and she reached for it without thinking. It was almost in her grasp when she stopped and withdrew her hand. She glanced down at the phone, then up at the inn and the dog before letting out a heavy sigh. If she was going to rest like the doctor ordered, she needed to unplug from the world—or at least from her world.

Eden picked up the phone and scanned the message. The issue was nothing major that needed her personal attention, so she forwarded it to her assistant. She trusted Fred. After all, she had trained him.

She reminded Fred that she wasn't to be disturbed unless it was an emergency, then reluctantly powered down the phone. She was officially unplugged. So, what was she going to do now?

Eden couldn't even remember her last true vacation. Not that this trip was really a vacation. *Vacations aren't forced on you.*

To remove the temptation of checking her messages, Eden left the phone in the center console. She had her own crisis to manage at the moment. Quickly, before she could change her mind, she grabbed her purse and slipped out of the car to greet her new furry friend.

"Well, aren't you adorable? I don't suppose you're here to carry my bags, are you?" Eden smiled at the shih tzu mix, who continued to wag his tail. "Okay, fine, but don't think I won't mention this to management."

The dog barked as if in protest.

Eden laughed while she retrieved her suitcase from the trunk.

Before she could make it all the way to the porch with her suitcase and dog in tow, the front door opened.

A woman with wavy brown hair and a warm smile stepped outside. "Welcome to the Magnolia Harbor Inn. You must be Eden Masterson."

Eden nodded.

"I see you've met Winston, and I'm Grace Porter, one of the owners." The woman took Eden's suitcase. "Come on in, and we'll get you settled."

"Thank you." Eden followed Grace into an immaculate foyer with white marble floors, a crystal chandelier, and enough warmth to make the bed-and-breakfast feel like a home. She breathed in the perfume of pink and white roses that tinted the air. It might not be a five-star hotel overlooking the ocean like Eden normally preferred and had almost booked, but she'd bet her life savings that this place was exactly where she needed to be to rest and get back to normal.

"Your inn is beautiful," Eden remarked. "And it's so quiet."

Grace's gentle laughter was like a melody. It instantly made Eden smile and put her at ease.

"Thanks," Grace said. "It's a quiet week with Thanksgiving coming up. The Miller family is still staying with us, but don't worry. Their teenage daughters are very sweet. They'll be checking out tomorrow morning. So it'll be only you and one other guest until next weekend. We're expecting her to arrive soon."

Another woman—younger and blonde but with the same warm smile as Grace—joined them and set the basket she was carrying down on the reception desk. The woman was slightly out of breath when she said hello to Eden, then gave the dog a stern look.

"This is my sister, Charlotte Wylde," Grace told Eden. "She's the other owner of the inn."

Charlotte held out her hand and gave Eden her full attention. "Welcome. It's nice to meet you. I'm sorry about that. I don't usually scowl at a guest. It was solely for Winston, the little scamp. He stole my muffin and took off on me."

"What?" Grace bent down to get eye level with the dog. "Winston, you know better. What's gotten into you?"

Winston barked.

Charlotte grinned and leaned down to scratch the dog's ears. "I guess it was too much for him to resist."

"Normally, he's a very well-behaved dog," Grace told Eden. Then she turned to her sister. "Maybe you should put Winston in my quarters."

"No, please don't," Eden said. "At least not on my account. Winston has been the perfect host since I arrived." She smiled. "Or he would have been if he'd carried my suitcase."

All three women laughed, making the dog bark with excitement.

Charlotte picked up Winston to cuddle him, and the dog licked her chin. "Even though he's a lousy bellhop, he makes up for it in love. Don't be surprised if he joins you on the veranda from time to time."

"I wouldn't mind that at all," Eden said, reaching out to pet Winston.

"We've put you in the Dogwood Suite, which overlooks the lake and has a fireplace and a private bath," Grace said.

"It sounds wonderful," Eden said.

Back to business, Grace checked Eden in. "The weather is supposed to be mild for the next few days. It will be great for exploring the area or getting out on the lake. Feel free to use our rowboat or one of the kayaks."

Eden had always wanted to try kayaking, but per her doctor's orders, she wouldn't be participating in strenuous activities anytime soon. Instead, she'd be sitting in a chair and watching the world pass her by. After years of living life in the fast lane, she honestly didn't know if she could transition to a slower pace.

"Things around town are a little slow at the moment," Charlotte said. "But the first Magnolia Harbor Holidaze Festival is coming up. You should join us. It'll be a lot of fun."

"It sounds nice," Eden said. "But what I really need is quiet and rest."

"You can get plenty of that here," Charlotte replied. "It's lovely sitting by the lake."

"Or out on the veranda," Grace added. She handed Eden a key to her room. "We serve breakfast but not dinner. However, we do have a nightly wine, cheese, and hors d'oeuvres hour at six on the back veranda." She motioned to her sister. "Charlotte is an amazing chef."

Charlotte set Winston down and picked up the basket she'd been carrying when she first arrived. "If you're searching for a good restaurant, I recommend The Tidewater on the other side of the lake. Dean Bradley is the owner and chef. He's a great cook, even if it pains me to admit that." She grinned. "Although I'm better."

The aroma of apples and spice hit Eden's nose when Charlotte lifted the cloth and offered her a mini muffin. Her stomach rumbled, reminding her that it had been several hours since breakfast, and as usual, she'd skipped lunch.

The muffins looked good, but she shouldn't indulge. Muffins were filled with fat and sugar, and now they were on the off-limits list. The doctor had told Eden to stick with heart-healthy foods. She had no idea what that really meant. With her constant on-the-go lifestyle, she'd never had to worry about her weight. Until her recent episode, she'd had no idea there was anything wrong with her. Hopefully, her new diet included more than bland chicken, celery, and carrot sticks.

"Thanks," Eden said, "but I don't want to ruin my appetite for those delicious hors d'oeuvres your sister mentioned."

"No worries," Charlotte said. "If you change your mind, the muffins will be on the table in the dining room."

"I hate to ask and be one of those demanding guests," Eden said, "but could you make the food heart-healthy?"

"Oh sure, that's no problem," Charlotte answered. "We can accommodate any dietary needs and restrictions. Are there any others I should be aware of?"

"No, but that feels like so much. Will food still taste good? My doctor tells me I have to give up all fatty foods and those with sugar." Eden grinned. "I'm pretty sure the man is trying to torture me."

Charlotte laughed. "You don't need fat and sugar to make food taste good. A little goes a long way and can still be all right for most people. If you'd like, I could share a few tips with you."

Eden had never been much of a cook, but now seemed like the ideal time to change that. "Do you think you could also teach me to prepare a few staple recipes to get me going? I'd pay extra."

"I'd be happy to and at no extra charge," Charlotte replied.

A phone rang at the reception desk, and a woman walked through the front door.

Charlotte excused herself to answer the phone.

Grace waved to the new arrival. "I'll be with you in a moment," she said brightly. She turned back to Eden. "Let me show you to your room."

"I'd like to take a look around first," Eden said. "Please go ahead."

"Thank you. Please tell us if you need anything." Grace moved to greet the other woman.

Eden stepped into the living room to explore her temporary home. The room was formal but warm in neutral shades of cream, with floor-to-ceiling windows and a gorgeous view of Lake Haven. Eden could easily imagine spending an evening in front of a roaring fire with the water twinkling beyond the lawn.

As the scene played out in her head, she let out a small chuckle. Who was she kidding? A whole evening of lounging? Maybe an hour tops before she started bouncing off the walls.

Snippets of conversation drifted in. Like Eden, the other guest, Jenna Salzman, was staying at the inn for the week. But unlike Eden, Jenna lived about an hour away in Charleston. It seemed odd to Eden that a young woman like Jenna would be vacationing alone and that she'd select a location she could easily drive to in such a short amount of time. Something told her there was more to Jenna's story than a simple vacation.

Maybe Jenna was running from something or someone. Not that it was Eden's business. Thanks to her job in public relations, specifically putting out fires due to her clients' poor decisions, her suspicious mind always jumped to the worst conclusions first.

Charlotte poked her head into the room. "Oh, there you are. Grace had to step away for a moment, and I'm here to show you and Jenna to your rooms."

By the time Eden rejoined the other women at the front desk, Charlotte had already picked up her suitcase and had one hand on the detailed iron railing leading up the curved staircase. She introduced Eden and Jenna.

Eden guessed that Jenna had to be somewhere around thirty. She had pulled her dark reddish-brown hair into a messy knot, and her green eyes were filled with anguish. *Yep, definitely more going on than a little getaway.*

"Do you need a hand, dear?" someone asked from the front door.

Charlotte smiled at the newcomer. "Thanks, but we've got it. Eden Masterson, Jenna Salzman, this is my aunt, Winnie Bennett, who lives nearby. Eden and Jenna are staying with us for the week."

Winnie clapped her hands in front of her. "You simply must join us for the Magnolia Harbor Holidaze Festival. It's going to be wonderful, and there will be something for everyone. I heard from Pastor Abrams that there's going to be a dance Friday night."

Eden's spirits plummeted even further. She loved to dance, although it had been ages since she'd cut loose. She doubted the doctor would approve of her breaking out her dancing shoes, but she was very tempted.

"There's also going to be a baking competition, an arts and crafts contest, a kids' talent show, and a dog show," Charlotte said.

"Will you be entering Winston?" Jenna asked. "He's such a sweetie, and I can tell he's intelligent."

Winston yipped.

"We were thinking about it," Charlotte replied. "But unless they're giving blue ribbons for best snuggles, I don't think he'd win."

All the women laughed.

"I'd be happy to train him this week," Jenna offered. "I work in a veterinarian office, and I have a knack for teaching dogs a few tricks."

"That would be terrific," Charlotte said. "Maybe you can train him to bring in the guests' bags, like Eden suggested earlier. Then we could get him one of those cute little bellhop caps to wear."

They all laughed again, which boosted Eden's spirits. She might not get to cut the rug on the dance floor, but she had a feeling it was going to be a good week after all. In the last five minutes, she'd laughed more than she had in a month. It was a sad and sobering thought.

The doctor had ordered her to rest, to find some balance in her life, to take up a few hobbies that would decrease her stress. He hadn't said anything about not living. A little dancing and boating couldn't be that bad as long as she took it easy, right? If she sat around all the time, she'd die of boredom. Maybe Eden could use her time in Magnolia Harbor to find a hobby that wasn't stressful.

And maybe the heart attack that had brought her to this point was her second chance at life. She kept that thought in mind as Charlotte showed her to her room.

Eden stepped into the Dogwood Suite and glanced around. It was lovely, with a gorgeous view of the lake.

But as she unpacked her suitcase, she couldn't help but think, *Now what?*

2

Charlotte

Charlotte loved to sing with the choir at the Fellowship Christian Church. She never coveted solos, but she had performed more than her fair share of them. Even so, she still got nervous. All eyes would be on her. If only she and Grace didn't have to alternate Sundays for church so someone could tend the inn. Charlotte always felt more confident when her big sister was in the audience. At least she had Aunt Winnie and Uncle Gus as well as her friends to lend her moral support.

The choir launched into the first verse of *Amazing Grace*, and Charlotte stepped forward, preparing for her solo.

Winnie smiled and gave her a thumbs-up for encouragement, and Gus nodded and waved. Bless her family for always being there for her.

Out of the corner of her eye, Charlotte watched Mimi Beale, the choir director. Mimi gave her the signal. Charlotte opened her mouth to sing, but the lyrics stuck in her throat as her gaze collided with a pair of distressed brown eyes in the last row.

Dean Bradley.

She was surprised to see him here. Not that he wasn't welcome, but Charlotte couldn't remember the last time she'd seen him in this church.

Mimi cleared her throat and signaled again for Charlotte.

Now was not the time to get stage fright. Charlotte closed her eyes and let the music take over her soul.

When her solo and the choir were done, Charlotte returned to her designated spot.

Pastor Glen Abrams stepped up to the pulpit. He thanked the choir, his kind eyes landing on Charlotte for a moment before he turned to face the congregation. The man was thin and wiry, with a head of white hair that resembled Einstein's. He was one of the most compassionate people Charlotte had ever met.

"As many of you know, I'm a Cardinals fan," Glen said. "Coming from Missouri, this should be no surprise. As many of you also know, I have a younger brother. Well, much to my family's surprise, my brother is a White Sox fan. We're not sure, but there is a running bet that Roger may have been abducted by aliens."

The congregation laughed at the good pastor's joke.

But Charlotte's attention was on the last row. Dean didn't laugh. His shoulders slumped. His head hung low. Gone was the stylishly dressed, confident—sometimes overly so—charming man Charlotte knew.

When Dean glanced up, his eyes were filled with pain and confusion.

Charlotte's heart squeezed, cutting off her breath. What could be going on with Dean that he'd seek solace in church? They'd known each other for a long time, and she'd seen many faces of Dean—happy, serious, arrogant, and even angry. But she'd never seen him looking like a scared child whose whole world had been ripped away in the middle of the night.

Glen's voice penetrated Charlotte's thoughts long enough for her to catch a few words about family, forgiveness, and love.

As Dean stared at the pastor, his face crumpled. Then he ducked his head and let his gaze fall to the floor.

Charlotte wondered if something had happened to Dean's family. She knew his parents were retired and lived in Florida and his brother and family resided in Atlanta. She said a prayer that his loved ones were safe and well. Whatever was going on with Dean, it was clear that he needed a friend. She decided to seek him out after the service.

Pastor Abrams finished his sermon on the importance of forgiveness, not only for the good of the one who had wronged you but for yourself and your own sense of peace. It was a topic she knew well given her past with Dean.

After the service, Charlotte hurried to catch up with Dean, but she was intercepted by her family.

"You did a wonderful job." Winnie's eyes lit up with pride.

"Thank you," Charlotte said, tamping down her impatience to get to Dean. "I'm so glad you were both here. I don't know why I still get so nervous about solos, but seeing you in the audience made all the difference in the world to me."

"You did give us pause for a moment," Gus admitted. "We thought maybe you'd forgotten the words." He chuckled. "I should have known better. You did a real fine job."

"I wanted to make sure I had everyone's attention." Charlotte winked at her uncle and then glanced toward the pews. Dean was still slumped there with his head down. "I should get going."

"You're planning to stick around and help with the festival preparations, aren't you?" Winnie asked. "Several volunteers had to leave early, and we need more people to sort the prizes."

"I'll be there," Charlotte answered. "I checked with Grace this morning, and she promised she had everything handled at the inn. The Millers checked out today, and Eden and Jenna checked in yesterday."

"How are they settling in?" Winnie asked. "I'm worried about Jenna. I can tell she's got something weighing on her mind."

"You ought to leave the young woman alone," Gus gently chided his wife. "She's here on vacation."

"I'm not bothering her," Winnie said. "I'd never do something like that."

Charlotte had to hold back her laughter at her uncle's expression.

They both knew full well that if Winnie thought someone needed help, she'd get involved somehow. Her aunt was a fixer. She was driven by a need to see those around her happy and healthy, and she would do anything to ensure it.

"I have one thing I need to do," Charlotte said, changing the subject. "And then I'll meet you in the basement."

Winnie glanced at Dean in the back row of pews. Concern filled her bright eyes. Her smile dimmed, and she patted Charlotte's shoulder. "Take your time. I'm going to see if I can round up a few more volunteers."

Charlotte walked quietly to the back of the church and took a seat next to Dean without speaking.

After a few moments, Dean let out a deep sigh and met her gaze.

The sight shocked her. His eyes were bloodshot and wet. This was definitely not the man she knew. "Hi," she said gently.

"I enjoyed your solo."

"It wasn't my best performance."

"Are you kidding? You were amazing."

Charlotte wouldn't go that far, but a small part of her warmed at his praise and the admiration she'd heard in his voice. "Thanks."

They sat in companionable silence for a few minutes while Charlotte tried to figure out how to ask him what was wrong.

"What's a nice guy like you doing in a place like this?" she asked finally, keeping her tone light.

Dean laughed bitterly. "Isn't this where you come to get answers?"

"Yeah, it is. Is there anything I can do?"

"Say a prayer." Dean shrugged. "Can't hurt, right?"

"Can you tell me who or what I'm praying for? Or is it more like a generic prayer for strength and goodness?" Charlotte held her breath as she waited for his answer. *This can't be good.*

"My mom." His voice cracked, and his whole body deflated.

"What's wrong?" she asked, then said a silent prayer that Dean's mother would be okay. When Charlotte had worked with Dean at Le Crabe Fou in Charleston, she'd met his mom. While Dean was outgoing and somewhat arrogant, his mother was one of the sweetest and most down-to-earth women Charlotte had ever known.

"They think she has cancer," Dean said, his voice wavering as he forced the words out. "She called this morning to tell me."

"Oh no. I'm so sorry." Having lost both of her parents, Charlotte understood his feelings only too well, although thankfully, neither of her parents had suffered through cancer. "But wait a minute. You said they *think*. That means they don't know for sure and there's a chance she's okay, right?"

"Yeah. She's having a test done tomorrow. A biopsy that will tell us for sure."

"When is your flight?" she asked.

For a few moments, Dean said nothing. He stared out the window, obviously lost in his own thoughts.

Perhaps he hadn't heard her. Or maybe he didn't feel like talking anymore. She should let him do what he came to church for, but she couldn't bear the idea of leaving him by himself.

"If you'd rather be alone, I can leave," Charlotte said. "Or if you want company, but you don't want to talk, I can do that too." If Grace were here, she would say the right things to make him feel better. Her sister had a knack for knowing exactly what people needed to hear.

"Please stay. I need to get this out." Dean took a deep breath and rubbed a hand over his face. "I want to fly there, but my mom said not to. She was adamant that I stay home and work until we know more." He shook his head. "Most of the time she's easygoing and sort of quiet, but when she gets an idea, she can sink her teeth into it like a dog with a bone."

"Well, being the only female in a house with three males, I'd imagine she learned to pick and choose her battles wisely and that she didn't lose often."

"Try never. I don't remember her ever raising her voice during an argument." He chuckled. "She simply wore you down with common sense and facts and pure stubbornness."

Charlotte couldn't help but smile. She sounded like the perfect mom for a guy like Dean. She paused before asking, "Has she been sick recently?"

"Not that I know of. I mean, she sounded like her normal self on the phone."

"That's a good sign," she said. "If she does have cancer, then they've probably caught it early."

"Yeah, that's what I'm hoping." Dean paused, then whispered, "I can't imagine my life without her."

It had been years since Charlotte had lost her mom to complications from pneumonia and her dad to a heart attack. Not a day went by when she didn't think of them both and miss them.

"I know it's hard to sit around and wait for results, especially when you're so far away, but you need to remain positive," Charlotte said. "Think of her stubbornness, her strength, and her faith. I'm betting she's not the type to go without a fight. Plus, they've made so many important strides in medicine these days."

"You're right, but I'd feel better if I were there with her," Dean said. "Unfortunately, she thinks it's a waste of money to come now and doesn't want me to take time away from work."

"So go anyway," she urged. "It's not like you'll be able to focus on work when you're worried about her."

Dean stared at her like she'd grown an extra head. "Are you crazy? Sick or not, if I showed up after she told me not to, I'd be in the doghouse."

"My mom used to tell us not to borrow trouble before it showed up on our doorstep," Charlotte said. "It's probably easier for your mom to put the pending tests and results out of her mind if life goes on as normal instead of everyone sitting around waiting."

Without saying a word, Dean suddenly took her hand in his.

Stunned, Charlotte gaped at his hand. It was scarred from cuts and burns just like hers—a byproduct of working in a kitchen—but it was so much bigger and stronger. She didn't want to think too much about how nice their hands fit together. This was Dean Bradley, the man who drove her crazy more often than not. They were completely incompatible, and right now what he needed more than anything was a friend.

They talked about life in general, business, and the upcoming town festival. The whole time he kept a tight grip on her hand. Charlotte had no idea how long they sat there. It could have been five minutes or an hour.

Snatches of conversations floated into the church. Children laughed while their parents talked to neighbors and friends. Winnie rounded up volunteers to sort prizes for the games they had scheduled for the festival.

Charlotte should be down in the church basement working, but being here for Dean seemed more important. He had lapsed into silence, his eyes closed. Charlotte continued to sit with him and silently prayed for his mom to be healthy and Dean to be strong. She also prayed for the wisdom to know how to help.

"Do you think she's going to be okay?" he asked.

She searched for the right answer, finally going with the truth. "I don't know, but I hope so."

"Thank you for being honest and sitting with me."

"Well, it was this or go back to the inn and scrub bathrooms,"

Charlotte joked, forcing a smile. "Actually, if you want to return the favor, you could join us in sorting prizes for the festival."

"For a second, I thought you were going to ask me to scrub the inn for you." He gave her hand a squeeze and let go before standing up and shoving his hands into his pockets. "I'd like to help, but I need to return to The Tidewater and get ready for the lunch crowd."

"Of course." Charlotte stood too, unsure if she'd done much good. She wondered what else she could say that would make a difference. "If you need anything . . ."

"Short of a time machine to make the next couple of days go by faster, I'm not sure there's anything anyone can do," Dean said. "But thank you for listening."

As Charlotte watched him walk out of the building, she said another little prayer for herself, because this vulnerable Dean was too likable. This softer, more accessible person was someone she could even see herself becoming close friends with.

Whether that was a good thing or not remained to be seen.

3

Jenna

There was nothing like autumn in the South. It was Jenna's favorite time of the year. Brilliant blue skies, orange and gold leaves on the ground, and crisp, cool air. The only thing missing was the smell of her mom's baking. With the extended family's early Thanksgiving gathering only a week away, her mom's kitchen would soon be a beehive of activity. Jenna should have been there, but instead she'd run away.

Who runs away at the age of thirty-one?

Me.

Jenna loved her family, every last one of them, but she couldn't take any more sympathetic looks or careless whispers. If she heard Aunt Lenore call her a "poor little lamb" one more time, she'd scream.

Jenna had considered staying home and playing sick, but that wouldn't have worked because her sister, Isobel, was a nurse.

No, there were no other options. The only recourse she could see was to lie about her whereabouts. As far as the family knew, Jenna was in Virginia for the week attending a course on emergency veterinary services.

What they didn't know was that the class had been rescheduled, and Jenna had chosen to slip away to a quiet inn in South Carolina rather than face them. She needed space and time to herself, and this seemed like the best place to get both.

Jenna felt miserable about avoiding her family, especially Isobel, who was not only her sister but her best friend. Not to mention that filling her time for the next seven days would be a challenge, but she'd find a way.

Earlier she had spent some time teaching Winston how to wave hello, spin in a circle, and then take a bow. He was a quick learner, but it would take more practice until he mastered the tricks. Working with Winston had been enjoyable, but it left her feeling restless.

It was such a beautiful day that Jenna started walking. Before she knew it, she was in downtown Magnolia Harbor. She ambled around for a while, excited to see that the town boasted a bookstore and a museum. But she still felt too keyed up to explore them. After noting the hours for The Book Cottage and the Jackson House Museum, she decided to come back later to check them out. She certainly had enough time.

As Jenna continued strolling the small downtown district, she stopped and glanced around. What was she doing? She had always considered herself an extrovert who relished exploring new places and making friends. But not now. She was an empty shell, unsure of everything. She needed to talk to her sister, but she couldn't call her. Isobel didn't understand. No one in her family did.

Of course, none of them had found out at the age of thirty-one that they were adopted either.

It wasn't even the adopted part that bothered her. Jenna knew there were many valid reasons why women gave up their children. Honestly, she was thankful that her biological mother had given her the chance to have a great life with the Salzmans.

Nope, it was the lie she couldn't accept. Betrayed by those who claimed to love her.

Maybe that was why Jenna was standing on a corner of a strange town feeling lost. She really hadn't had a plan when she'd started her walk, but when she noticed a steeple, she had an idea of where she needed to go.

Jenna hesitated in front of the church. Should she go in? She didn't want to disturb the morning service. She'd seen a movie where the new girl in town walked in during the middle of the sermon. The door squeaked, and everyone in the church twisted around to stare at her.

A shudder ran through Jenna at the thought. That would be just her luck.

Maybe she'd hang out on the sidewalk until everyone exited the building. Or maybe she should return later. But she didn't want to seem like a church stalker. There was a café in town. She could grab a coffee and figure out a game plan to get through the week.

As she contemplated what to do, the doors opened and people spilled out of the church. Couples and families mingled on the front lawn, no doubt catching up after the service.

Jenna edged closer, not wanting to intrude yet seeking the comfort of others, of belonging. Except these weren't her people—not her friends and definitely not her family. She didn't belong here. She didn't belong to anyone really, and that stung.

"This is a waste of time," Jenna muttered as she started to turn away.

An older man with wild white hair stepped outside. Next to him was a younger man of average height with broad shoulders and short brown hair.

Jenna was struck by the younger man's pale-blue eyes. There was kindness . . . and love when he looked at the older man and the woman who had joined him. They were probably his parents.

A small pang of longing tugged at her heart. Jenna missed her family and the easy camaraderie they'd had, the open dialogue they'd shared her whole life. She hoped they'd find their way back there someday.

Perhaps the pastor could give her some tips. As she was deciding if she should interrupt the group and ask to speak to the pastor for a moment, she noticed a familiar blonde waving to her. It was Charlotte.

Jenna made her way to the group, where Charlotte introduced

her to Pastor Glen Abrams, his wife, Penny, and their nephew Cole Briggs—aka Mr. Blue Eyes.

"What brings you to our little town?" Penny asked Jenna.

Outright lying to a pastor and his family seemed wrong on multiple levels, but Jenna didn't want to get into the reason why she was here either. "I'm getting some alone time and a break from the city before the craziness of the holidays."

"Well, you picked the perfect week to visit," Penny said. "We're hosting our very first Magnolia Harbor Holidaze Festival."

"Charlotte told me all about it when I checked in yesterday," Jenna said. "It sounds like a lot of fun, especially the dog show. I'm excited about anything to do with animals."

"Oh, speaking of the dog show," Charlotte said, "was Winston a good boy for you this morning?"

"He was the best," Jenna answered. "He's a smart guy."

"Did you teach him any new tricks?" Charlotte asked.

Jenna nodded. "He's off to a great start, but he needs more practice. I want to make sure he's got the tricks down before I show you and Grace."

"Are you a dog trainer?" Cole asked. "If so, I've got a Jack Russell terrier who could use some pointers."

"There's nothing wrong with your dog," Penny said. "She's got you right where she wants you: wrapped around her front paw."

The group laughed.

Jenna faced Cole to answer his question. Making eye contact with him was like staring at a warm, sunny sky. "No, I'm a veterinarian technician, but I'm pretty good with dogs. Jack Russell terriers are intelligent but very stubborn."

"That's an understatement," Cole said with a grin.

"I'd offer to work with her, but that might be a conflict of interest since I promised Charlotte that I'd get Winston ready for the competition." Jenna leaned over to Cole and staged-whispered, "But I could probably give you a few tips."

"Thanks," Cole said. "I'll take all the help I can get."

"Speaking of help, do you have some free time?" Glen asked Jenna.

Everyone turned to her. It was that squeaky door scene come true. Jenna cleared her throat. "Why do you ask?"

Charlotte laughed and patted her arm. "Don't worry. We're only going back into the church to set up for the festival."

"Oh, I'm so sorry," Jenna said. "I didn't mean to interrupt your plans. It was nice meeting all of you."

"You're more than welcome to join us," Glen said. "We can always use another set of hands."

Jenna knew she should say yes, but she held back. They were only being nice. "I should return to the inn. I didn't even tell Grace I was leaving. I wouldn't want her to think I fell in the lake or something."

"Nonsense. I'll send her a text and let her know you're here with me," Charlotte said. "We could really use you. We're short-staffed."

"Not to mention that I have no idea what I'm doing," Cole added.

Jenna wavered for another moment. She didn't have anything planned for the rest of the day, and she'd noticed that Cole hadn't taken his eyes off her. She had to admit that his attention sent a little thrill zinging through her. "Okay."

"Wonderful," Glen said. "Let's get to work."

Jenna followed the others into the church and down to the basement. Before she knew it, she'd been handed a box, assigned a table, and paired up with Cole to sort toys.

"Do you do this often?" Jenna asked as she removed a stuffed bear from the box and dropped it onto the table.

"Do what?" Cole asked.

She smiled. "Pluck unsuspecting visitors off the street and put them to work."

"My uncle doesn't believe in idle hands," Cole replied.

"Probably comes with the job." She tossed him a stuffed panda, then scanned the crowded basement room. "Looks like he's winning the battle. What about you? How do you keep busy other than being at your dog's beck and call?"

"I have my own landscaping business in Charleston," he said.

Jenna hesitated as she reached for a stuffed bunny. She'd figured Cole for a hometown boy. "You live here and work in Charleston?"

Cole shook his head. "I live and work in the big city, but I regularly visit my aunt and uncle. The rest of our family's in Missouri."

"It's nice that you visit. Do you miss the rest of your family?" Jenna couldn't imagine being so far away from her parents, let alone her sister. Yet here she was distancing herself during one of the biggest family holidays of the year.

"I do, but I don't miss the cold. I came to South Carolina years ago on a family vacation and didn't want to leave. My folks and my younger sister will be out for Christmas. What about you? Where's home?"

"Charleston," Jenna admitted.

He grinned as he opened another box. "Not big on getting far away, are you?"

She could lie and say her apartment was being fumigated or something, but there'd been enough lying to last a lifetime. "It was sort of a spur-of-the-moment decision. But think of it this way—no plane ticket to buy, no long lines to get through security, and chances are I won't get seasick."

"You make some good points," Cole said with a chuckle.

Charlotte stopped by with cups of hot chocolate and a plate of cookies, including Jenna's favorite—snickerdoodles.

Jenna and Cole continued to talk as they ate, sorted prizes, and tested out games for the upcoming festival. She found out Cole lived only a few blocks from her. They'd probably crossed paths or at least had near misses at the grocery store, the gas station, maybe even the park. It was funny how life worked.

"Thank you for helping us out today, Jenna. We all appreciate it. And, Cole, it's always good to see you."

Jenna glanced up from her task of threading fishing line through miniature fishing poles to see Winnie, Charlotte's aunt. "I should be thanking all of you. I had nothing planned today, and this has been a lot of fun." She glanced Cole's way. He was watching her with a warm smile, and she instantly felt her cheeks heat.

Cole winked at Winnie. "You're lovelier every time I see you."

"Now you stop that," Winnie said, her eyes twinkling. "Anyway, I have something for you," she said to Jenna and handed her a black pool ball.

No, it wasn't a pool ball. As Jenna turned it over, she discovered it had a little window. It was a Magic 8-Ball. "What's this for?"

"I thought it might help you," Winnie said.

"Help me with what?" Jenna asked. She loved the gift, but she was completely perplexed as to why Winnie would give it to her or how it could help.

Winnie patted her hand and winked. "I don't know. When I saw it, I knew I had to give it to you." With that vague answer, she walked away, leaving Jenna and Cole staring at the odd toy.

"I had one of those when I was a kid," Cole remarked.

"So did I," Jenna said. "My sister and I would get its advice on everything. We'd ask it what to wear and if some boy liked us."

He grinned. "Oh yeah. How was its accuracy rate?"

Jenna laughed. "Well, I was awfully cute in my cheerleading uniform, but Robbie Cruz still didn't ask me to the prom. I give it a fifty-fifty."

"Did it say he would?"

"The reply was 'Without a doubt.'" Jenna sighed, remembering her teenage heartache as she ran her fingers over the ball. "Instead, he asked my friend Mia. Well, my former friend and now his wife."

Cole took the ball and shook it. "Maybe it misunderstood. *Me*. *Mia*. It sounds similar. You should give it another try."

"What should I ask?" She thought about it for a moment. "Dear Magic 8-Ball, will we ever finish sorting these prizes?"

Both Jenna and Cole watched the white die float around before rising to the top.

Very doubtful.

Jenna laughed. "It's right. If we don't get back to work, we'll never get done."

They worked in tandem for the next couple of hours, talking and laughing at the silliest things. Cole was laid-back and fun to be around. For the first time in weeks, Jenna's thoughts didn't revolve around her family drama. It was nice. Peaceful. Normal. She'd missed not being consumed with pain and turmoil.

"Hey, are you okay?" Cole asked.

Jenna startled, realizing her thoughts must have shown on her face. "Yep, I'm fine," she answered, then changed the subject. "Despite the Magic 8-Ball's prediction, we seem to have finished sorting toys."

Cole picked up the ball and shook it. "Maybe it'll be more accurate on the next question."

"What question is that?"

"Would it be too forward of me to ask Jenna out?" He flipped the ball over.

The die floated to the top. *Cannot predict now.*

"Maybe it's telling you to take a chance," Jenna said, holding her breath. Her stomach flipped in anticipation. She liked Cole, and if the last couple of hours were anything to go on, he might be the distraction she needed.

"Jenna Salzman, you are the most intriguing woman I have ever met. Would you do me the honor of having dinner with me Tuesday night?"

Yes! She screamed on the inside. "Hmm, let's see." She tried to play it cool as she watched the die rise to the window. A small smile tugged at the corners of her mouth when she read the answer.

Yes.

4

Eden

Monday morning, Eden rolled over in her very comfortable bed and glared at the glowing blue numbers on the alarm clock. It was five o'clock.

Why couldn't her internal clock have broken when her body had? But she already knew the answer. She'd spent too many years getting up at the crack of dawn even after hitting the pillow well after midnight. No wonder she'd had a heart attack. In retrospect, she was slightly surprised she'd lasted as long as she had. Thankfully, she had been given a second chance and still had time to correct where she'd gone wrong in life, although she might go crazy from the boredom.

It was dark outside, so Eden pulled the spare pillow over her eyes and tried to will herself back to sleep. For the next hour, she dozed, tossing and turning.

Finally, she gave up and got out of bed. What to do? It was too early for breakfast, and she didn't want to wake her hostess or Jenna.

Eden picked up the suspense novel she'd started reading a couple of days ago and settled down in the chair.

After rereading the same paragraph a few times, she tossed the book aside. What was the point? Eden would bet good money on how the book ended. The villain was the lead detective's partner who had been attacked years before by the victim.

Instead of wasting her time on the novel, she opted for a long soak in the bathtub.

An hour later, feeling refreshed but still restless, Eden headed downstairs for breakfast. She hoped she'd find something interesting to fill her day.

"Good morning." Charlotte stepped out of the kitchen with a carafe in one hand and a plate in the other. "I was just taking this out to Jenna on the back veranda. Can I get you something to eat or drink?"

Eden eyed the eggs Benedict with envy. Oh, how she loved the lemony-smooth flavor of hollandaise sauce, but sadly, she didn't think it was the best option for her health. "Some fruit and toast would be nice."

"Would you prefer a croissant instead of toast?" Charlotte asked. "How about Greek yogurt and decaf coffee too?"

"I can still drink coffee and eat yogurt and croissants?" Excitement coursed through her at the thought.

Charlotte smiled. "You bet."

"That's wonderful. Thank you." Eden followed Charlotte out to the veranda.

Charlotte delivered Jenna's meal and then excused herself to get Eden's breakfast.

"Mind if I join you?" Eden asked.

"Please do," Jenna responded. "It's beautiful here, isn't it? So peaceful and relaxing."

Eden sat down at the table. "Don't get me wrong, but it seems like an unusual choice for someone like you. Magnolia Harbor is lovely, but the pace is rather on the slow side." Not that South Carolina didn't have its own fascinating offerings, but when she was Jenna's age, she had traveled to large cities with fabulous shopping, an exciting nightlife, and rich cultural events.

"I could say the same of you," Jenna replied. "You strike me as the sort of person who is always on the go and would choose to stay in a bustling city."

A ping of disappointment ricocheted through Eden as Jenna's comment hit a bull's-eye. If she'd taken this vacation of her own volition, where would she have gone?

Without a doubt, she would have flown to Paris. She hungered for a fresh croissant and a decadent cup of coffee while sitting at a charming outdoor café on the banks of the Seine.

"Maybe I was searching for a change of pace," Eden said.

Before Jenna could reply, Charlotte returned with Eden's breakfast—fruit, yogurt, a croissant, and a cup of decaf coffee.

Suddenly the day was better. While Eden may not be in Europe, she had everything she needed: a beautiful inn set on the banks of Lake Haven with the sun shining down and good company.

Charlotte handed Eden the plate. "Enjoy."

"Thank you. That's exactly what I was craving," Eden said. "Do you think after breakfast we could start my cooking lessons?"

Charlotte's shoulders dropped, and she frowned. "I'm so sorry, but I have to run a few errands today. We could start tomorrow morning if you're free. You could help with the appetizers for social hour."

"That sounds good." Now if only Eden could find something to do until tomorrow. "Do you have plans for today?" she asked Jenna.

The younger woman finished the last of her breakfast and nodded. "I'm working with Winston on some new tricks this morning."

"Oh, that's right," Eden said. "He's a contestant in the dog show on Saturday."

"And he's going to be fabulous," Jenna assured them. "After that, I'm going shopping downtown. You're welcome to join me."

"I'd like that," Eden said. It certainly beat reading the predictable book in her room.

Charlotte excused herself, and Eden and Jenna settled on a time to meet for their trip into town. Then Jenna went to find Winston, leaving Eden alone on the veranda.

Out of habit, Eden glanced around for her cell phone to check messages and e-mail. She was surprised when she didn't see it on the table. Then she remembered she'd left the phone in her car for moments like this. Eden considered running to the car to get the phone, but she quickly dismissed the idea.

She needed to learn how to relax. After all, it was part of the reason why she was on this vacation.

Instead of thinking about work, she sat back and sipped her decaf coffee, then took a bite of the croissant, intentionally focusing on its buttery flakiness. The sun glinted off the lake, and in the distance, a few brave souls were out fishing. Closing her eyes, Eden listened to the birds sing and enjoyed the breeze on her face. Maybe she could get used to this slower pace.

After breakfast, Eden took her dirty dishes to the kitchen. She hadn't seen Grace yet, and she didn't want to let the food residue sit and harden, so she washed the dishes herself and set them in the drying rack, since she didn't know where to put them away. It was nice to lose herself in the simple task.

Watching the fishermen had given her an idea. Instead of returning to her room where utter boredom awaited her, she headed outside with the intent to explore. As long as she took it easy, she should be okay.

Winston came bounding up to her as soon as she stepped outside.

Bending down, she scratched the adorable dog's ears and scanned the area for Jenna. "Shouldn't you be in doggy pageant class right now?"

Winston barked and turned in a circle before sitting down in front of her.

Eden laughed and clapped. "Good boy. Is that one of your new tricks? If so, the judges are going to love you."

The dog barked again and ran down the stairs to disappear around the side of the inn.

Eden followed him. "Maybe I'll take a walk around the lake," she mused.

"You might want to rethink that plan," Grace said from where she knelt by one of the glorious flower beds. "The lake has 285 miles of shoreline."

Winston yipped and wagged his tail.

Grace dropped a handful of cut flowers into a basket beside her. "However, there is a nice trail that leads to a beautiful spot under an old oak tree that's great for reading or watching the wood storks catch fish."

Eden sighed. More sitting around? She'd have to pass. "Those are lovely flowers," she remarked.

Grace picked up the basket. "I'm refreshing the floral arrangements. Normally, Charlotte or my aunt joins me, but they're not around this morning. I'd love some company if you're not ready to take a walk yet."

"Sure, but I must warn you that I'm no good at floral design." In home economics a long time ago, she'd tried. The teacher had taken one look at Eden's centerpiece, clucked her tongue, and deemed it *interesting*.

"Perfection is overrated," Grace said as she walked to the kitchen.

Eden and Winston trailed her.

The dog immediately plopped down on the floor.

"It seems that Winston is ready for a nap. He must be tuckered out from his lessons." Grace smiled, then set the basket in the middle of a center island. "Can I get you a cup of coffee or some tea?"

"I would love some," Eden answered, "but the doctor warned me to cut out caffeine. I'll have decaf."

"Can I ask what happened?" Grace poured a cup of coffee for Eden and gave it to her.

"Heart attack." Eden lightly rubbed her palm across the center of her chest, remembering how she'd gasped for air as if she'd run up a flight of stairs but had been sitting at her desk. She never wanted to experience that kind of fear again. "Thankfully, it was a mild one."

"That must have been terrifying." Grace took a pitcher of iced tea from the refrigerator and poured herself a glass. Then she placed a couple of vases on the island next to the basket, gently pushing one in front of Eden.

"Hopefully, you'll never have to find out for yourself, and I'll never have to go through it again." Eden picked up a red flower and stuck it in the vase. "At first, I didn't understand what was happening. It was nothing like you hear about or see on TV."

"What was it like?"

"One minute I was fine, and the next my lungs stopped working. Then I broke out in a cold sweat. I thought I was having a hot flash."

"Those I understand." Grace selected several flowers, cutting each at different lengths before effortlessly and artfully arranging them in the vase.

A dark thought clouded Eden's mind. What if her assistant hadn't found her in time? Would she have survived? Shoving the horrible questions away, she forced a smile and chose a few more flowers.

"I imagine having something like that happen makes a huge impact on your life," Grace said. "Not only on the mental level but also the physical limitations."

"The doctor explained that I'd have to take it easy with physical activities, but in a few weeks, I should be fine." Eden paused. "The biggest impact for me is the need to eliminate the stress from my life. With my job, that's nearly impossible."

Grace took a sip of iced tea. "What kind of work do you do?"

"I'm in public relations. Basically, I'm the fixer. When our clients get themselves into some kind of trouble that will affect their reputation or make their company stocks crash, I step in and clean up the mess."

"Sounds like an interesting job," Grace commented.

Eden smiled. "It is, and I enjoy it. Plus, I'm good at putting out fires. However, it's a job that keeps you hopping. I tend to get up early and go to bed late. Most meals are at my desk or as I'm running out the door. It's not exactly the healthiest lifestyle."

"I completely understand. I used to work at Maddox Creative as the vice president of new business development."

"Another stressful job." Eden fussed with the flowers in her vase, moving them around without much success. "Why did you leave?"

"I was working way too many hours," Grace replied.

"Was it difficult transitioning from a corporate job to owning an inn?" Eden asked.

Grace stuck a white rose in the middle of Eden's vase before taking a long sip of her tea. "Not really. It should have been. I loved my job at the company, and I was there for nearly twenty years. But I also love what I do here. I stay busy, and it's interesting meeting guests. Not to mention it gives me much more time with my family."

"That does sound like a wonderful trade-off." Eden studied her work as she turned the vase around and around. At least the arrangement was symmetrical.

They continued discussing life in the corporate world, marketing, and public relations.

Grace slid another vase in front of Eden while she tinkered with the mess Eden had made of the first. Every now and then, Grace would shift a flower in Eden's bouquet, never saying a word or losing her patience with Eden.

They talked more about Grace's switch to a less demanding career and how she stayed engaged. Eden was enthralled with Grace's tale, the light of excitement that shined in her eyes as she talked about the inn and working with her sister.

Could there be something like that out there for Eden?

She'd never done anything else. After college, she'd gone straight to Bergman Relations, where she had worked her way up to executive communications manager. What else would she do? What could she do? It might be time to explore her options.

"Those are lovely," Grace said. "And we're done."

Eden regarded the flowers in front of her. They were pretty and didn't look like something a toddler had put together. She glanced up at the clock and was surprised to find a couple of hours had passed. "This was fun."

Maybe not in the same adrenaline-pumping league as public relations crisis management, but it was definitely less stressful. It was an activity she could see enjoying at home but not as a new career. Her skills were definitely not up to that level.

"Thank you for your assistance and company," Grace said. "I really should go tidy up yours and Jenna's rooms. If you want something else low-key to do, there are some wonderful shops in town, like Spool & Thread. Winnie meets with her quilting group there every Tuesday at six. I'm sure they'd love for you to join them."

"I'm no good at sewing."

Grace laughed and pointed to the vases on the island. "That's what you said about floral arrangement, and I beg to differ. Just think about it, and if it's not your cup of tea, I think the book club is meeting at the library tonight."

Eden left Grace to get her work done and headed outside toward the lake. She smiled as the sun warmed her face. The time with Grace had left her feeling lighter, happier, and more like her old self. After a few days of rest, she was a new woman. Birds were singing overhead, lightening her mood even more. She glanced around to make sure no one could see her, then did a little song and dance routine, laughing. When was the last time she'd acted silly and carefree?

Too long ago.

And that was sad. Life didn't come with any promises. There were no guarantees that Eden would live a long time. She'd been issued a warning. It was time to start paying attention to life, because it zipped by faster than she expected and she didn't want to miss out on one more minute of it.

A sharp pain shot through Eden's side, stopping her in her tracks.

She pressed on her side and glanced over her shoulder. The inn was within sight. Actually, it was fairly close. She couldn't have gone more than half a mile. Yet with every breath, her lungs burned and squeezed.

"No, not again." She gazed skyward. "Give me a break, will You?"

Eden closed her eyes and focused on the signs her body was giving her. Yes, she was winded, but it wasn't like last time. That had been searing pain, and her lungs had shut down. This felt more like she'd sprinted a mile with no conditioning. The pain in her side was nothing more than a muscle cramp.

The doctor had warned her, but of course she hadn't listened. She'd felt a little better, had some energy, and thought she could pretend she was on a real vacation, not recuperation.

Leaning against the trunk of an old oak, Eden slowed her breathing and massaged the muscle. Why was this happening to her? One of her clients had suffered from a massive heart attack and flatlined twice on the way to the hospital. Not only had the man pulled through, but the doctor hadn't made him restrict his activities.

All she wanted was her life back. Was that too much to ask?

5

Charlotte

Charlotte parked her black Toyota Camry in the parking lot at The Tidewater and grabbed her purse. She hoped she wasn't overstepping her bounds.

Sleep had eluded her. Instead, she'd spent the night worrying about Dean. She couldn't forget the very real and deep pain she'd seen etched on his face at church. Having lost both of her parents, Charlotte understood the fear he faced. Thankfully, neither of hers had suffered through a long, drawn-out illness. But loss was still loss, and Dean was much too young to lose his mom.

The woman behind the reception desk glanced up as Charlotte entered the lobby of the small and trendy inn Dean owned. "Good morning. What can I do for you today?"

"I need to see Mr. Bradley," Charlotte said. "Is he in his office?"

The woman blanched, her gaze darting toward the restaurant. "He's in the kitchen. If you'd like, I can call back there and ask if he's free."

Charlotte waved her off. "No need. I'll pop in and see for myself."

The receptionist's eyes went wide, and she simply nodded.

That didn't bode well, but Charlotte imagined that Dean's staff must be worried about him too.

The first thing Charlotte noticed as she stepped into the closed restaurant was the lack of noise. Waitstaff scurried around as they set the tables and prepped for the lunch crowd, but no one said a word. A scowling waiter rushed by her with a tray of salt and pepper shakers. Other staff members cast furtive glances her way and exchanged a volume of thoughts with each other solely through body language.

Charlotte knew those looks. She'd worked in the restaurant business for a long time, and she was able to read the room like a well-loved book. The chef was in a mood and not to be trifled with.

"Can I help you?" asked a young woman setting a nearby table.

"I'm going to speak to Mr. Bradley," Charlotte answered. "The receptionist told me he's in the kitchen."

"That's right." She glanced at the set of double doors in the back of the room. "But be warned. You're entering at your own risk."

"Duly noted. Thank you." Charlotte smiled at the other staff members as she headed toward the cave of doom.

Dean wouldn't be the first bear she'd encountered in a kitchen. Charlotte had worked with several chefs who wore their arrogance, pride, and short tempers on their sleeves and took out every frustration on the staff. While Dean could be a bit arrogant at times, she didn't recall him ever being a demanding diva with the staff. If anything, Dean usually charmed his coworkers.

Unsure what she'd find, Charlotte poked her head between the double doors and scanned the room. Annie, the commis chef, busily chopped vegetables with her head down. Ruby, the sous-chef, was nowhere to be seen. And Dean stood at the sink with his back to the door.

"Hello," Charlotte called as she stepped fully into Dean's domain.

Dean glanced over his shoulder and frowned. "What are you doing here?"

"I wanted to talk to you," Charlotte answered.

He stepped to the side and turned off the water. "Give me a minute. I burned myself."

Charlotte noticed a red mark on his hand. That probably hadn't improved his temper. "No, stay where you are. Where's the first aid kit?"

"Over there." Dean pointed to a nearby cabinet.

Charlotte grabbed the kit, then set down the box and opened it before examining his hand. It was bright red and blistered. She was surprised that Annie was still blithely chopping vegetables instead of helping him. "You should see a doctor. That's at least a second-degree burn." Even though she was careful in the kitchen, she knew from personal experience how easily accidents happened.

"I'll be fine," Dean said shortly. "Besides, Ruby is going to be late. Right now it's just Annie and me, and we open for lunch in less than an hour. If this is about the Holidaze Festival, can we talk later when things quiet down?"

"It's not about the festival." Charlotte applied an anesthetic and antibiotic cream, then wrapped his hand in gauze. She snapped the kit closed and washed her hands. Grabbing a clean white chef's jacket off a hanger, she slipped it on.

"What are you doing?" Dean asked, confusion and amusement evident in his voice.

"Helping." Charlotte buttoned up the coat and gestured to his hand. "You need to keep that dry, and there's no way you can cook with it."

"Sure I can."

"Let me rephrase that. You shouldn't try to cook with that burn yet. Every time you bring it near the stove, you're going to be in pain." She put her hands on her hips. "Now tell me what you need done."

Dean stood his ground, glaring down his nose at her.

Charlotte understood his reluctance. It was hard for any chef to relinquish his kitchen to someone else. It was Dean's reputation on the line if she messed up. However, while she might have left the restaurant life, she was still a professional chef. She had the cookbooks to prove it, and she did her fair share of events at the inn.

They stood toe to toe for a good thirty seconds.

Finally, Dean sighed and stepped aside. "Today's specials are rustic shepherd's pie and bacon-wrapped turkey breast with cranberry compote and sweet potatoes." He filled her in on what he'd already finished.

"Good. Sit and make sure I'm doing things right."

Dean pulled up a stool so he could watch her work.

Annie brought over the onions and carrots, then went back to the potatoes she'd already boiled.

Charlotte took the skillet Dean had set aside when he'd burned his hand and returned it to the stove. "Where's your recipe card?"

He motioned to the shelf above her. "So, what did you come over to talk to me about?"

She retrieved the card and scanned it, then started sautéing the onions and carrots. "Have you heard anything else from your mom or dad?"

"Not yet." Dean ran his uninjured hand through his short hair. The fact that he did so in the middle of his kitchen said volumes for how distracted he was. All chefs knew not to touch their hair while handling food. If he was that upset, it was no wonder he'd gotten hurt.

"No news is good news, right?" Charlotte said.

"Whoever came up with that saying obviously never had to wait for important news," he snapped.

"I'm being nice to you, so the least you can do is return the favor," she said brusquely.

His shoulders slumped. "You're right. I'm sorry. Thank you for being here."

"Of course." She gave the pan a shake and reached for the lamb. "How are you doing?"

"I think I'm losing my mind." He rolled his shoulders and neck, then took a deep breath and let it out slowly.

Charlotte peered at him. Dark circles marred the skin under his eyes. "Did you get much sleep last night?"

Dean shook his head.

Restaurant work was demanding, especially for the owner and the chef. It involved long hours, late nights, and early mornings. Not just anyone could fill in, which was why her next suggestion would probably not go over well.

"You should fly down to Florida," she said, adding the tomato paste, chicken broth, and other ingredients. "That way, you can be there for your mom. It'll also make you feel better."

"I want to, but I can't," Dean said. "My mom said to stay home. Plus, I've got my duties here, and I'm working on the kids' talent show."

Charlotte could relate. Even though her life was fairly flexible these days, it was a rare treat when both she and Grace were able to leave the inn at the same time. If they did, Winnie stepped in to play hostess in their absence. But Dean didn't have that support system. He was a control freak when it came to his job, and he was all about presentation and his reputation. It wasn't necessarily a bad thing, except at a time like this.

What he needed was someone he could trust.

Charlotte switched off the heat under the skillet and turned to Dean. "Okay, I've got a crazy idea. You fly down to Florida, and I'll fill in for you here."

From his shocked expression, it was as if she'd suggested he serve store-bought marinara sauce and commercially made pasta at his restaurant.

When the seconds ticked by and he didn't respond, Charlotte started to get annoyed. Didn't he trust her?

"You've got your own business to run," Dean finally said, his deep voice soothing her ruffled feathers.

"We only serve breakfast, and Ruby can handle that meal here." She held up a finger before he could interject. "I can get the nightly appetizers for our social hour ready in the morning, and Grace can take care of the final touches and serve them to our guests. Besides, it's only for a couple of days, and the inn is kind of quiet this week."

Dean crossed his arms over his chest and leaned so far back on the stool that Charlotte thought he'd tumble over. "You're going to cook breakfast for your guests, prep your nightly appetizers, then hustle over here and handle the lunch crowd. Then in the short time between lunch and dinner, you'll take care of your festival responsibilities and mine." He shook his head. "It's too much for anyone, even you."

Charlotte had to bite her tongue. His words were like a gauntlet thrown down in a challenge, something she had a hard time walking away from. "Maybe the pastor's nephew Cole can take over the kids' talent show."

And while she didn't usually press her guests into work, she had a feeling that Jenna would be happy to lend Cole a hand.

"As for my responsibilities, the baking competition is all set," Charlotte went on. She grabbed the cranberries for the next dish to prep. "I got my judges weeks ago. There's nothing left for me to do there."

"It sounds like you've got it all figured out." Dean scratched his jaw that was covered by a meticulously groomed five-o'clock shadow, his dark-brown eyes filled with doubt. "Why would you go to all this trouble for me?"

His question threw her off-balance, and she spilled some sugar on the counter. "What do you mean?"

"You're offering to take time away from your business," he replied. "And before you start to argue, hear me out. I know you do more than cook breakfast and make fancy finger foods. You and Grace handle everything at your inn."

It was true that Charlotte and her sister ran the place between the two of them. They hired a service to take care of the expansive grounds and lawn, but otherwise they cooked, cleaned, manned the front desk, and played concierge, bookkeeper, manager, and even matchmaker and confidant for their guests. The two of them worked well together, and usually they could handle the demands of their inn without much outside assistance except for Winnie, who tended to show up right when they needed her.

"So why would you do this for me?" Dean asked.

It was a good question. She hadn't stopped to see Dean with any grand plan in place. She had simply wanted to check on him. Did he think she was trying to insert herself into his business? They'd had their issues in the past but had worked through the problems. Sure, they still had a friendly competition going on as to who was the better chef. He had won first place for his dish at the Strawberry Festival contest, and she had her best-selling cookbooks. But she didn't think it was mistrust that made him ask.

She struggled to find the words to explain.

Dean kept staring at her, waiting for her answer.

He seemed to be hinting or digging at something he wanted her to confess. Something she wasn't ready to admit out loud, especially with his already overinflated ego. Something she barely allowed herself to recognize—that she liked him.

Shrugging, with her focus on the stove and the bubbling compote in front of her, she went with an old cliché. "It's what friends do."

After getting Dean through the lunch rush and confirming that Ruby would be in soon, Charlotte returned to the inn.

Winston greeted her at the door, then followed her to the kitchen.

Grace was pouring a glass of sweet tea. Before Charlotte could say anything, her sister handed her the glass and poured a second one.

Charlotte thanked her and took a sip. "I have some news."

"Oh, it sounds like I arrived just in time," Winnie said as she strolled into the room. She pulled out a stool and smiled. "I can't wait to hear this."

"It's nothing like that." Charlotte laughed. "I went to check on Dean, and I offered to take over for him at The Tidewater for a couple of days." She filled her sister and aunt in on Dean's family situation. If she was going to take time away from the inn and put more work on her sister, then she had a right to know why.

Both Grace and Winnie murmured their sympathies and promised they'd keep Dean's mother in their prayers.

Winnie reached over and squeezed Charlotte's hand. "You did the right thing. Your parents would be proud of you."

"Don't worry about the inn," Grace said. "I can handle things this week. Eden and Jenna are two of the least demanding guests we've ever had. Both are such a blessing. Eden arranged flowers with me this morning, and Jenna has been keeping Winston busy with his lessons." She smiled. "I almost feel like I should be paying them to stay here."

"Right now it's business as usual since Dean's not planning on going to Florida," Charlotte said. "Hopefully, he'll hear good news soon. But I wanted to give you a heads-up in case he needs to go."

"I appreciate that," Grace said, then took a sip of her tea.

"I'm glad Eden arranged flowers with you this morning," Charlotte said. "I hope it calmed her down. She seemed a little on edge during last night's social hour."

Grace nodded, her blue eyes clouding over. "If I hadn't had Jake, I imagine I would have been a lot like her after I lost Hank. Driven. Dedicated. Married to the job."

"Isn't she supposed to be resting?" Charlotte asked.

"I don't think she knows how," Grace said.

"How can we help?" Winnie asked.

"She's definitely a type A personality, so sitting around reading or watching the birds isn't going to work," Grace said. "I suggested that she check out the downtown shops."

"I could invite her to our quilting group tomorrow night," Winnie offered.

"I already mentioned that," Grace responded. "But she told me she's no good at sewing."

"I'll invite her anyway," Winnie said. "She might surprise herself and enjoy it."

"I'll be teaching her some basic recipes tomorrow morning," Charlotte said. "And the Holidaze Festival starts Wednesday, so that will give her more to do without creating any extra stress."

Winston whined.

Grace bent to pick him up. "I think Winston wants to help too."

All three ladies laughed and gave the dog a good scratch behind his ears.

"Now, what about Jenna?" Grace asked. "I'm not sure what's going on with her, but it's clear something is weighing heavily on her shoulders. She's fine when she's giving Winston his lessons, laughing and talking to him. Has she said anything to either of you?"

Both shook their heads.

"I know what you mean," Winnie said. "I saw her on the veranda on my way in, and she looked like a lost and frightened child. Of course, as soon as she saw me, she perked up."

"Maybe she had a bad breakup recently. It's always harder when the holidays are approaching and you're single." Charlotte let out a sigh. She'd tried to find love, but so far, all the nice guys had eluded her. "Although she did seem to hit it off with Cole Briggs."

"The pastor's nephew?" Grace asked. "He's very nice."

"I'm going to see if Cole can help with the kids' talent show," Charlotte said. "That way if Dean does fly to Florida, we'll have a backup director. Maybe we could even get Jenna to lend a hand, since she seemed to enjoy sorting toys with Cole yesterday."

"Playing matchmaker, are we?" Winnie asked, her eyes twinkling.

"No, just being a good friend and hostess," Charlotte said. "Besides, matchmaker is usually your job, and I'd never dream of trying to take it from you when you like it so much."

Winnie huffed. "I have no idea what you're talking about."

Both sisters smiled and wisely drank the rest of their sweet tea in silence.

6

Jenna

Jenna sat on the back veranda, sipping a glass of iced tea and watching a pair of wood storks fish in Lake Haven.

Eden had told Jenna that she wasn't feeling up to shopping with her, and Jenna had decided not to go either. What she really wanted to do was call Cole and invite him to go out on the lake with her. She asked the Magic 8-Ball what to do, but it told her to ask again later.

Why was she even turning to a toy for the answer in the first place?

She set the ball on the seat next to her and grabbed her phone. It was the twenty-first century, and she was a modern, independent woman. If she wanted to ask a man out, then she could.

But first she needed to quell the storm of butterflies in her stomach.

There was something incredibly sweet and old-fashioned about Cole. Something that said he was worth getting to know better, and maybe that was exactly why she couldn't wait to see him again. Granted, they'd just met, but deep inside, she knew he was one of the rare and elusive good guys.

Forgetting what the Magic 8-Ball advised, Jenna scrolled through her phone contacts until she came to Cole's number.

Right before she could call him, her phone rang. It was Isobel.

Jenna picked up. "Hey, how's it going?"

"Well, things could be better," Isobel said, then launched into a rant about work.

Jenna sat back and listened to her older sister, adding the much-deserved noises of sympathy when needed and laughter when called for. If Jenna thought being a veterinarian technician was tough, it was a cakewalk compared to Isobel's job as a registered nurse. Isobel put in long, stressful, heartbreaking hours, but she loved what she did and her patients loved her.

When Isobel finished her rant, she asked, "So, will you be here for the family dinner?"

"No, I won't be home Saturday."

"I can't believe you're missing it," Isobel said. "You have to come."

Jenna rolled her eyes. "We've already been over this. I need the class to get a promotion."

It wasn't a total lie. She needed to take the class her family thought she was taking this week. And it did mean she'd get a promotion at work once she completed the program. It was a great opportunity. In addition to a pay raise, it would allow her to specialize in assisting with canine and feline eye surgeries. She loved her job and her patients as much as her sister loved hers, but Jenna's patients were the four-legged variety.

Jenna didn't want to lie to her family, and she hadn't started out lying to them either. She had been scheduled to take the class this week, which was perfect timing to get her out of the family get-together. Then the class had been rescheduled for early next year.

She was going to tell her family about it until she'd run into Aunt Lenore at the grocery store. To listen to the woman, it sounded like Jenna had been some stray puppy abandoned on the side of the freeway and rescued by her parents.

She could only take hearing "you poor little lamb" and "bless your heart" so many times before she blew up. So in reality, Jenna's fib was doing the family a huge favor and saving them from a dramatic scene at the dinner table.

At least, that was what she kept telling herself.

But Jenna felt awful lying to her sister. They'd always been the best of friends, but she knew if she were honest with Isobel, her sister would tell their mother, who would be crushed. Her mom would then tell her father, who would confront her aunt, and on and on it would go.

Families were complicated puzzles. Sometimes all the pieces fit together nice and snug. However, most of the time, there were a few pieces that didn't seem to fit quite right, but they got smashed in with the rest. Lately, she felt like the latter version.

"Are you sure you won't change your mind?" Isobel asked, breaking into Jenna's reverie. "Are you mad about what happened?"

"No, but I am hurt that Mom and Dad kept the fact that I was adopted a secret for so long."

Her sister burst into tears.

Jenna felt horrible. She wasn't trying to make her family feel bad, and she didn't doubt that they truly loved her, but she had a right to know. As a nurse, Isobel should understand that there were biological reasons why Jenna should have been told about the adoption.

"Please don't cry," Jenna said. "You're still my sister. Nothing can ever change that. But now I don't have to worry about wearing reading glasses like Dad when I'm older, and you still do."

Isobel laughed.

"Listen, this is just between us," Jenna said. "Sister Cone of Silence."

"Okay," Isobel said. "What is it?"

"I love you. I love Mom and Dad. I have the best family ever." Jenna chuckled. "Well, as long as you don't count the extended family. Some of them are absolutely bonkers."

"You've got that right," Isobel chimed in.

Jenna became serious again. "I want you to know that I'm not off searching for my biological parents."

Jenna didn't hate her birth parents or hold any grudges or ill will toward them for putting her up for adoption. If anything, Jenna owed them a huge thank-you for giving her not only a chance at life but an amazing life. Even so, Jenna had no intention of ever tracking down her biological parents. She simply didn't feel that urge.

What Jenna needed was for the hullabaloo to die down and life to return to normal. She needed her extended family to treat her as they had before. She needed time to finish processing the news, get her emotions in check, and figure out how she really felt. And most importantly, she needed to get past her own hurt and mistrust and feel like she belonged again.

But the road to normal wasn't paved with a gazillion sympathetic people shoving pie in her face. Not that pie wouldn't help soothe some of those hurt feelings.

Her sister cleared her throat, bringing Jenna's attention back to their conversation.

"Sorry," Jenna said. "I'd better go."

Isobel snorted. "All right, I'll talk to you later." She hung up.

Sighing, Jenna tossed her cell phone on top of her sweater as Grace and a man with salt-and-pepper hair stepped outside with Winston and a chocolate Lab in tow.

"This is our neighbor Spencer Lewis," Grace said to Jenna, then motioned to the beautiful Lab with them. "And this is Bailey."

The dog sat down in front of Jenna and wagged her tail.

Grace turned to Spencer. "Jenna has been teaching Winston a few tricks for the dog competition. She's Winston's new best friend, and I think he might try to stow away in her suitcase when she leaves."

Winston barked as if in agreement, and they all laughed.

"If you want to head down to the shed, I'll be there in a minute," Grace told Spencer. "All the tools to fix the loose door are inside."

"Sure." He signaled to Bailey to follow, but she whined and gazed longingly at Jenna.

Jenna laughed. Winston was already in her lap. "It's okay if she stays. I love dogs."

"Thanks. Bailey likes to hang out with Winston." Spencer took the steps two at a time and headed off.

Grace sat down in the chair next to Jenna, scratching Bailey's ears. "I think she also senses when someone needs a friend. Both dogs do. Am I wrong?"

Jenna snuggled Winston closer while reaching out to pet Bailey. "No, you're not. Animals are the best kind of therapy. They make you feel better simply by being around. Plus, they're great listeners. It's a shame they can't give advice."

"I may not be as cuddly," Grace said. "But I am a good listener, and I have occasionally been known to give good advice."

Jenna needed to talk to someone, but she didn't want to bother Grace. She was her hostess, not her confidant. She was sure Grace had more pressing matters to attend to. If Jenna weren't mistaken from Spencer's expression, he was hoping Grace would join him in fixing the shed door. "It's nothing. Just sister drama."

Grace chuckled softly. "Believe it or not, that is something I know a little bit about."

"Really? But you and Charlotte seem so close." In a way, the two innkeepers reminded Jenna of her and Isobel.

"We are, but that also means we know which buttons to push to get a response."

Jenna groaned in agreement. "Exactly. Isobel is an expert button pusher."

"I'm betting you're the same," Grace said with a grin. "Ask her or your parents."

At the mention of her parents, guilt washed over Jenna, which was exactly what Isobel had been aiming for.

Grace reached out and rested a hand on Jenna's arm, then gave it a gentle squeeze. "I'm sorry if I said something that upset you."

"No, please don't apologize," Jenna said. "My sister and I are having a disagreement. She's the type that needs to confront it head-on and get it over with right away. But I need time to process."

"And she doesn't like to give you the time you need," Grace said.

Jenna shook her head. "Isobel doesn't believe in a cooling-off period. She says that only gives the argument time to fester and poison your heart."

Jenna's pain must have been radiating off her in waves. Not only did she have Winston in her lap, but Bailey settled at Jenna's feet and rested her head on them. At the rate Jenna was going, both dogs would soon be sitting in the chair with her.

Grace glanced at the dogs and smiled. "You don't strike me as the type to hold a grudge. I'm guessing your sister's need to confront the problem right away comes from the need to make sure that the problem hasn't created a long-term issue between you. To reassure her that you two are all right."

Bailey nestled closer to Jenna's ankles and sighed.

Grace held out her arms for Winston.

But Jenna waved her off. "They're fine. It's like having a weighted blanket. You're probably right about Isobel. She's a caregiver, a nurse. So she's always worried about everyone around her."

"That makes a lot of sense."

Charlotte stepped outside with a pitcher of iced tea and stopped with a look of surprise on her face. "Are we having a puppy snuggle party and no one told me?"

"I think Winston and Bailey have adopted Jenna as one of their own," Grace said.

Jenna winced at Grace's choice of words, but she forced a smile.

"Your sister and the dogs have been cheering me up as I monopolized their time. You're welcome to join us. We were talking about sisters and drama and pushing buttons." She grinned, hoping to lighten the mood.

Charlotte refilled Jenna's glass with iced tea and then sat down. "Well, let me just say that whatever Grace has said is all an exaggeration. I am and have always been the perfect little sister."

All three ladies laughed at that statement, with Charlotte laughing the hardest.

Once Charlotte caught her breath, she leaned back and studied Jenna. "In all seriousness, is there anything we can do to help? I don't mean to be pushy, but we hate to see anyone sad."

"Oh, I'm not sad," Jenna replied.

Both sisters nodded, then glanced at each other.

"I suddenly feel like I got two more big sisters." At their concerned faces, Jenna rushed to assure them it wasn't a bad thing. "You've both made me feel welcome here. So have Winston and Bailey. I really appreciate the sympathetic ear and advice, but I need time to deal with the issue and regain some sense of normalcy in my life."

Charlotte shot Grace a mischievous grin and then quirked her brow at Jenna. "If you've got some free time on your hands, I know of a good way to fill it."

Warmth spread through Jenna. The last time Charlotte had put her to work, she'd met Cole Briggs. Maybe whatever Charlotte had in mind would put her back in Cole's radius. "I've got all the time in the world," Jenna announced. "What can I do for you?"

Charlotte gave a little squeal, making Winston sit up and bark with excitement. "Thank you. You're a lifesaver."

Grace rose, and Winston jumped down to stand next to her. "I'll let you two discuss Charlotte's idea while I go see if Spencer needs any help with the shed. Jenna, if you need anything, let us know."

"I will," Jenna said. "And thank you for the advice."

After Grace and the dogs left, Jenna asked Charlotte, "So how can I help?"

Charlotte explained that a friend of hers was in charge of the kids' talent show at the festival, but he might have to leave town on a family emergency. "I'm going to find out if Cole can pitch in this weekend, and I was wondering if you'd like to as well. If we had a backup or two, then it would make things easier for Dean if he needs to leave in a hurry."

Guilt warred inside Jenna. She wanted to assist Charlotte. The sisters had been so nice to her since arriving at the inn, and her parents had raised her to help out others in times of need. Not to mention it would be nice to spend more time with Cole. But her sister's words were eating away at her. What was she supposed to do? Stay and help out strangers, respecting her parents' teachings? Or go home and be with her family, putting them first?

"What do you think?" Charlotte asked.

"Normally I'd say yes," Jenna responded. "But I have some family stuff going on, and I don't want to commit to something that I might not be able to do. Besides, I have no idea how to run a talent show for people. I'm better with dogs."

"No worries. I understand. It was only an idea," Charlotte said. Then her eyes lit up. "I'm sure Cole will be glad to help, especially if he knows that you'll also tentatively be there . . ."

Jenna laughed. "You're not very subtle."

"You said you needed some normalcy in your life," Charlotte reminded her. "There's nothing more normal than spending time with a handsome guy who's interested in you. Contributing to a great cause at the same time is a bonus."

Jenna lifted her glass and saluted Charlotte. "I think we're going to be wonderful friends."

7

Eden

Tuesday morning Eden woke up in time to watch the black of night slip away as the sun rose over Lake Haven. The sky turned a beautiful reddish orange and then faded into bright blue. Another perfect day in South Carolina. A day that beckoned her to explore the great outdoors and the sparkling waters and do things her doctor and body warned her not to do.

"Lovely," she muttered. "Why couldn't it be raining cats and dogs?"

According to her bedside clock, she'd slept for twelve straight hours. The last time she'd done that was when? Her teen years? Maybe earlier.

It didn't matter because Eden was listening now. She'd learned her lesson. Yesterday had shown her how easy it was to overdo things physically. She needed to learn to pace herself and do better. Her stomach rumbled, reminding her that she'd skipped dinner and now was the ideal time to start making changes in her life.

After a quick shower, Eden dressed in jeans and a light sweater and headed downstairs. She followed the aroma of coffee to the kitchen. She gave the door a tap and pushed it open.

Grace and Charlotte were sitting at the island with cups of coffee in front of them.

"Good morning," Eden said. "I'm sorry for interrupting."

"You're not interrupting," Grace said. "Would you like a cup of decaf coffee?"

"Yes, thank you," Eden said.

Grace got up and poured a mug of coffee, then handed it to Eden. "I'll let you two get to work on your cooking lesson. Enjoy."

Charlotte picked up her own mug. "Before we get started, I'd like to ask you a few questions about your current routine and likes and dislikes."

"Sure." Eden sat down next to Charlotte. "Ask away."

"How much cooking do you do now?"

"Absolutely none." Eden hesitated. "Unless you count coffee and toast."

Charlotte smiled over the rim of her cup. "It's a start. Okay, other than coffee, bread, and I assume butter, what else is in your refrigerator and pantry? What are your staples?"

Eden pictured her nearly bare cupboards and hardly used appliances. She was almost too embarrassed to admit their sad state of affairs. "An assortment of cheese—gouda, a sharp cheddar, and probably a brie. Occasionally some grapes or berries, bottled water, and a crisp white wine. And there are usually crackers in the pantry along with the bread."

"Anything else?" Charlotte asked.

"A can of soup and a box of macaroni and cheese," Eden admitted. She couldn't recall when she'd bought them, and she was willing to bet they were well past their expiration dates. Honestly, they were only there in case of an emergency.

Charlotte rubbed her thumb along the edge of her coffee mug before setting it down and grinning at Eden. "The good news is, you can keep most of it."

"I can?" Eden asked.

"The cheese will have to be eaten in moderation due to the high fat content. And there's actually some new research that says white wine might be just as heart-healthy as red, so you're good there as long as you drink it in moderation. Let's see if we can expand your fruit selection and add some veggies, along with lean proteins. Also, we'll want to exchange the butter for olive oil and get you cooking at home. Does that sound overwhelming?"

"Not at all."

Charlotte laughed. "You and Jenna may be my two favorite guests of all time."

"You probably say that to all the guests," Eden teased.

"Yes, but I actually mean it this time," Charlotte said. "I like how you're not backing down from a challenging situation."

"So, where do we begin?" Eden asked.

"I thought I'd show you a few quick and easy breakfast recipes this morning. The first one is a no-bake bar. You can make it on Sunday and then grab one on your way out during the week. They're healthy, tasty, and simple."

"It sounds great."

"Here's the recipe." Charlotte set an index card on the counter and pointed out where the ingredients were located while she poured herself another cup of coffee.

Eden followed all the steps, asking questions when she wasn't sure of an ingredient—like agave nectar—and if she could swap out raisins with something else. She was pressing the ingredients into a pan when Grace popped back into the kitchen with Winnie.

"Oh, yum. No-bake bars." Winnie poured herself a cup of coffee and took a seat at the island. "But those aren't raisins. What did you use instead?"

"Dried cherries and blueberries," Charlotte answered. "Eden doesn't care for raisins."

"That will be a nice change," Winnie said.

"I agree," Grace said. "By the way, Jenna is up. She doesn't want anything heavy for breakfast today. Maybe some fruit and yogurt."

"I've got an idea," Charlotte said. "A banana split."

All three women stared at her.

Charlotte laughed. "Relax. It's for breakfast, and it's the next recipe I'm going to show Eden." When they all kept staring at her, Charlotte rolled her eyes and reached into the refrigerator. "Yogurt."

Eden's shoulders slumped. "You had my hopes up for a minute."

Winnie reached over and patted Eden's hand. "Mine too."

"While you indulge, I'm going to take care of Jenna's room," Grace said, and she slipped out of the room.

"Would you like to join us for breakfast?" Charlotte asked her aunt.

"No thank you. I ate with your uncle this morning. However, I am curious as to how you make a banana split with yogurt."

Charlotte handed Eden the recipe card and got out two long bowls. Together they cut the bananas in half, lengthwise. Next, they scooped out vanilla Greek yogurt and placed it on top. Then they warmed up raspberry preserves and spooned them over the yogurt and bananas. Finally, they sprinkled fresh blueberries and sliced almonds on top.

Now if Eden could add fresh whipped cream it would be perfect.

While Charlotte took Jenna's breakfast out to her, Eden sat at the kitchen island with Winnie, enjoying her creation.

"How is it?" Winnie asked.

"Excellent." Eden smiled. "Even if it doesn't have whipped cream."

"Leave it to Charlotte to show us such a fun treat," Winnie said.

"I'm grateful she agreed to give me some lessons in the kitchen. When the doctor told me I had to start eating healthier for my heart, I thought I was doomed to tasteless and boring food. In one morning, Charlotte has proven that isn't the case."

"You should check out her cookbooks," Winnie suggested. "We have copies of them for sale in the foyer. You'll never have to prepare another dull meal in your life with those in your kitchen."

"I'll do that, especially since I don't want another heart attack. If I don't start making some serious changes in my life, that's exactly what's going to happen."

Winnie smiled at her. "I'd say you're on the right path. Charlotte can help you with the eating healthy part, and it sounds like you've figured out the rest on your own."

"Not really," Eden said. "All I do is work. I don't have any friends outside of work. No life outside of work. No hobbies. Nothing. I need to find a way to unwind. As it is, I'm going stark raving mad sitting around doing nothing."

Eden winced at the confession. What was wrong with her? Normally she kept all her thoughts and emotions firmly locked up. In her business, loose lips sunk ships and empires. But here she was spilling her guts to a complete stranger. She didn't know if it was Winnie's innocent eyes and sweet smile, or if she'd drunk enough of the small-town magic juice and had started to think like the locals.

"What have you done since you arrived?" Winnie asked.

"Yesterday I helped Grace with the flower arrangements, which was nice. But afterward, I tried to go walking around the lake and overdid it." Eden scooped up the last of her banana split and licked the spoon. It was so good she could see herself eating one daily. "Jenna and I had planned to go shopping, but I was too exhausted from my walk and had to cancel."

"My quilting group, The Busy Bees, is meeting tonight at Spool & Thread at six," Winnie said. "You're more than welcome to join us. There's not much physical exertion, but there's plenty of social interaction."

"I might visit the museum today and take you up on your offer too. Thanks." Eden didn't know a thing about sewing or quilting.

Then again, she hadn't thought she'd be much good at flower arrangements either, but according to Grace, that had turned out pretty well.

After a morning of successful cooking lessons, Eden drove into town to explore Magnolia Harbor properly.

First, she stopped at The Book Cottage, where she met the owner, Blanche Townsend. Or in her mind, Hurricane Blanche. Eden had intended to buy one book. She told Blanche that she wanted something fun to read before she fell asleep at night. But Blanche showed her so many intriguing books that Eden couldn't choose only one.

Thirty minutes later, Eden walked out with a historical fiction on Thomas Jefferson's daughter, a woman's fiction about two sisters, a book on learning American Sign Language, and a book on meditation. Well, she did love history, she'd always meant to learn ASL, and the others would be good for her health. At least that was her story, and she was sticking to it.

Between the heart attack and her stay in Magnolia Harbor, she was becoming a whole new Eden Masterson. The old her wouldn't have let a stranger tempt her with so many books. Instead, Eden would have marched into the store, gone straight to the thriller section, and grabbed a book. No deviating. No browsing. No stepping outside her comfort zone.

But the experience hadn't been scary or even uncomfortable, as she would have expected. It had been freeing. She'd have to remember that.

After exploring a few other quaint shops on Main Street, Eden stopped at the Dragonfly Coffee Shop.

A lovely young woman with beautiful olive skin and gorgeous henna artwork on her hands took her order.

"I'll have a decaf tea. Do you have any low-fat muffins?" Eden asked. She'd been very good, but after walking around town, she was a bit on the ravenous side.

"We have a mixed berry muffin that's made with applesauce instead of oil," the woman said. "Personally, it's one of my favorites."

"That sounds delicious," Eden said. "I'll take one."

The woman returned with her order within minutes. She'd even warmed up the muffin.

"Thank you," Eden said. "By the way, I love your henna."

"Thanks. It's one of my many art forms—everything from painting to quilting."

"Oh, Winnie Bennett invited me to Needle & Thread tonight for quilting. Will you be there?"

She laughed. "I think you mean Spool & Thread. Yes, I will. I'm Angel Diaz. Have you done much quilting before?"

Eden glanced around and then lowered her voice. "Never. Is that okay?"

Angel laughed again. "It's fine. We love newbies and getting them hooked on crafting. There's something magical about expressing your creativity in a solid, physical object that you can enjoy for years to come."

"I never thought of it that way," Eden said. "Is there anything I should bring?"

"An open mind and lots of patience." Angel smiled, then excused herself to greet the customers who had just walked in.

Eden was surprised to find she was actually getting excited about the evening's activities.

As she sat there sipping her tea and munching on the delicious berry muffin, she couldn't help but overhear the conversation between the two women at the table next to her. The women owned their own craft business—homemade soaps and candles as well as jewelry—but were lamenting about how slow business had been lately.

"I really hope this Holidaze Festival is worth our time," one of the women said.

"Why wouldn't it be? We did well at the last craft fair we went to."

"True. It's feast or famine. Business is great during the holidays and summer, but what about the rest of the year? I still have to feed the kids during the off-season. We need a steady income. Jimmy says I need to find a paying job, and if I do that, I won't have time to work with you."

Eden could see the pickle the woman was in. She could only burn the candle at both ends for so long. Working two jobs while taking care of her kids and a husband was like lighting both ends and burning the middle at the same time.

Eden swung around in her seat. "Excuse me. I'm sorry for interrupting, but I couldn't help but overhear. You ladies are entrepreneurs and are here for the festival. That's fabulous. I'll have to make sure I stop by your booth."

"Please do," one of the women said. "Look for the Serenity Boutique."

"What a lovely name for a store," Eden remarked.

"That's what we thought too," the woman said. "Unfortunately, we haven't been able to open a storefront yet. We're from Charlotte, and the rent is too expensive for us."

"Sadly, that's true for too many," Eden said. "Do you sell online?"

"We've tried," the other woman answered, "but we don't get much traffic."

"Would you mind a few suggestions?" Eden asked.

"We'd love to hear them," the first woman said.

"You might post some pictures of your products on social media sites. It's all the rage these days." Eden named a few sites for the ladies to check out as well as a few for them to avoid.

Eden ended up spending a good hour talking with cousins Louise and Addie about low-cost marketing for their business.

At the end of their chat, Eden felt exhilarated to have put her brain to work again. Except this had been different. There had been no stress. No tightening of her chest. No burning in her stomach. Only good old-fashioned pleasure and pride in helping these women out.

The ladies had offered to pay Eden for her advice. She had refused. That was a no-brainer. They hadn't sought her out for assistance. She had offered. It was a good deed, and she was pretty sure she had benefited more from the chat than they had.

8

Charlotte

Thanks to Eden, Charlotte managed to wrap up her morning chores in the kitchen sooner than she'd expected. Surprisingly, her guest turned out to be not only a fast learner but also eager. Eden was now equipped with several breakfasts and lunch recipes, and that night's appetizers were prepped and just needed to be popped into the oven.

Now Charlotte was headed to the church to talk to Pastor Abrams. She was going to ask him if his nephew could assist Dean with the kids' talent show.

She parked her car in the empty church parking lot and grabbed the plate of cookies she'd made especially for the pastor. They were peanut butter with cranberries and white chocolate chunks.

Charlotte smiled as she took a moment to regard the classic white clapboard church with steeple. She always felt at peace here. Her boots crunched on the gravel walkway as she made her way around to the back of the church through the gardens to the pastor's office. It was a beautiful spot, and a giant magnolia tree filled the area with its glorious scent in the spring and gave them shade in the summer.

She knocked on the door, then let herself in and called, "Hello?"

"In my office," the pastor replied.

She found him at his desk, hair sticking up, tapping a pencil on a yellow legal pad.

"What's another word for *provoke*?" Glen asked without glancing at her.

Charlotte thought for a moment. "Incite?" she suggested.

He threw his pencil down and quickly typed something into his phone before smiling at her. "Thank you. I've been stuck on that one for the past five minutes."

"Working on this weekend's sermon?" she asked.

"No, I'm embarrassed to admit. It was a crossword puzzle challenge from my nephew. But that does give me an idea." Glen set the phone down and eyed the plate of cookies she was holding. "Are those for me?"

Charlotte grinned. "Now who else would I make peanut butter cookies with cranberries and white chocolate for?"

"Thank you so much," he said. "But I'm assuming you didn't stop by just to drop off cookies. Is everything okay at the inn?"

She handed him the cookies, then took a seat and stared at the floor. Asking for help should be a simple task. But the reasons behind the need were not her story to tell, and Charlotte didn't want to betray Dean's trust. She'd already told Grace and Winnie, but she reasoned they needed to know why she was taking time away from work and asking them to cover for her. Plus, they were family.

Of course she had nothing to worry about. The pastor wasn't the type to blab the secrets of Magnolia Harbor's residents.

"Life at the inn is good," Charlotte said. "It's been kind of quiet so far this week, but we have two lovely ladies staying with us. You've already met Jenna Salzman."

"Yes, she was a big help on Sunday. I hope we'll be seeing more of her." He smiled. "My nephew seemed quite taken with her."

"She's wonderful," Charlotte agreed. "Winston is very much in love with her as well, so Cole already has some competition."

Glen laughed.

"Our other guest is Eden Masterson," Charlotte continued. "Jenna and Eden are both so nice and easygoing that it's like having friends instead of guests visiting."

"Good. So I'm guessing you're here for another reason."

She nodded. "It's about the festival. I was wondering if Cole could help Dean with the kids' talent show. Dean has been very busy and could use some assistance."

"I'll give Cole a call," he offered. "If it gives him a reason to be in town where he can see Jenna, then I have a feeling that he'll say yes."

"I think you're right," Charlotte said with a laugh.

Glen leaned back in his chair and studied her. "Are you okay? It seems like you've been taking on a lot of things at once. Remember, it's okay to say no."

"What do you mean?" she asked, surprised.

"You're in charge of the baking contest, and you and Grace have both been pitching in with setting up the children's games and ordering prizes and supplies." He sat forward, resting his hands on the desk. "It's not that we don't appreciate the work you're doing. You've got such a generous heart and soul, but I worry about you."

"What about me?" Charlotte asked. This wasn't the reaction she'd expected at all.

"You're always giving of yourself to others," Glen replied. "When do you find time for yourself?"

"Don't worry. I'm taking plenty of time for me," Charlotte assured him. It was true that she had a lot on her plate, but she would rather be busy than bored, and she enjoyed making other people's lives easier.

After chatting for a few more minutes about the festival, Charlotte left Glen to enjoy the cookies.

With that task done, Charlotte drove to The Tidewater to check in with Dean. Hopefully, he'd heard some good news about his mother. But if not, maybe the prospect of Cole assisting with the talent show would put him a little more at ease. It might even convince him that they had everything covered here in Magnolia Harbor and he could fly to Florida to be with his mom.

When the receptionist saw Charlotte, she pointed to Dean's office door and motioned for her to go on back.

Charlotte knocked on the door. She waited, but Dean didn't respond. After a few moments, she continued on toward the kitchen.

As during her previous visit, staff members were setting up the dining room for lunch, except today the mood was considerably lighter. Several greeted her, but most went about their business as if Charlotte's presence was a regular occurrence.

Charlotte stuck her head around the kitchen door but didn't spot Dean. It seemed odd that he would be absent so close to opening the restaurant. Maybe he'd stepped into the cooler?

She glanced around and saw Ruby at the counter, cutting vegetables, and approached her. "I'm looking for Dean. Can you tell me where to find him?"

"He's not here," the sous-chef answered. "He asked me to take over for lunch."

"He did?" Charlotte asked, feeling her pulse speed up. *His mom.* It was the only explanation why a control freak like Dean would leave his kitchen in someone else's hands. He must have gotten bad news and left.

After thanking Ruby, Charlotte rushed outside to the patio to call Dean. He needed to know she was pulling for his mom and also that she was there for him if he needed to talk. She reached into her purse and came up short when she noticed Dean sitting in an Adirondack chair, gazing at Lake Haven. Charlotte's heart sank.

He didn't turn around as she walked over to him.

For a few moments, Charlotte simply stood, quietly taking in the serene beauty surrounding them. It was early in the day, yet the sun shone overhead and made the water's surface sparkle and glitter. The trees were late to shed this year, and they were still bathed in orange, red, and gold. During the summer, the lake was filled with fishermen, boaters, and children playing at the water's edge, but today even the ducks were absent. It was only the two of them.

"Mind if I join you?" Charlotte finally asked.

"We're not open for lunch yet, but I have an in with the chef if you're hungry." The humor in Dean's words didn't reach his eyes or even his smile.

She sat in the chair next to him. "How bad is it?"

"I don't know." Dean ran his fingers through his hair, blowing out a deep breath.

"Talk to me," Charlotte said.

"I waited but didn't hear anything this morning. Finally, I called my mom, who sounded shocked that I was calling." He faced her. There were dark shadows under his eyes. "Am I not supposed to care because I'm a man?"

"Of course not," she said firmly. "You know that's not what your mother meant. She probably figured work would have kept you busy all morning and that you wouldn't have a chance to call until after the lunch crowd."

Dean didn't respond. Instead, he focused on the lake.

"What else did she say?" Charlotte asked.

"Nothing really. That she'd call when she heard back from the doctor and that these things take time." He snorted. "Then she asked what today's special was."

Charlotte couldn't help but smile, which was probably the wrong thing to do because that made Dean stare at her as if she'd lost her mind. "Sorry. But it sounds like a question your mom would ask."

"It is." Dean pushed himself to his feet and started pacing. "Under normal circumstances, it's exactly what she asks me during every one of our conversations. What's today's special? What's new on the menu?" He crossed his arms over his chest. "Who cares what the special is?"

"She does." Charlotte stood up and met Dean's eyes. She could see all the pain, the struggle, and the suffering she'd gone through with her own parents' deaths. Dean lived hours away from his family, and she hated that he was enduring this turmoil alone. When she'd lost her parents, she'd had Grace right there with her, as well as Winnie and Gus and many other supportive family members. "Your mom is scared."

"She didn't sound scared."

"Of course not. She's your mom. She has always guided you and set an example. She doesn't want you to be afraid, so she's going to hide her own fear to make you feel better. I saw my mom do the same thing."

"But even my dad and Marc seem to have this relaxed attitude about the whole thing," Dean said. "Like it's no big deal. Dad was out golfing. How could he do that? I don't understand."

"Come on. Let's take a walk." Charlotte led him down a path along the lake and through the trees. She hoped a stroll would expel some of his nervous energy.

"I'm losing my mind," he said. "I can't stop worrying, and the rest of my family is acting like it's a debate over what color to paint the living room."

She nodded. "For some people, living in denial is the easiest way to deal with stressful situations. But I simply face whatever life throws at me head-on. I've never allowed myself to live in denial."

"Don't take this wrong, but you're lucky."

Charlotte gently bumped his shoulder and smiled. "I am."

They were silent for a few minutes as they ambled down the path.

"I haven't been able to stop thinking or praying for good news about your mom," Charlotte said softly.

"I appreciate that." Dean bent down and picked up a couple of flat rocks, handing one to her. "The thing is, I'm also worried about my dad if the tests come back positive. If my mom doesn't make it, how will he survive? They've been together so long. I don't even think my dad knows how to make a bowl of cereal."

"You don't know the biopsy results yet," Charlotte reminded him. "I realize it's easier said than done, but try not to worry about that right now."

"It's hard not to worry." He chucked his rock across the lake, getting it to skip two times.

Charlotte tossed her stone and tamped down on her pride when it hit the third skip. Now was not the time for their competition to surface. On second thought, maybe it was exactly what he needed to bring a bit of his normal life back into focus. "Looks like I got you beat on rock skipping."

The comment hit the mark as Charlotte had hoped. Dean dug around for more stones. "You got lucky that time."

For the next few minutes, a friendly rock-skipping contest ensued. It was a close call that had them both grinning and laughing with Dean winning by half a skip.

"Ha!" he crowed triumphantly. "Gotcha!"

"I'm reserving the right for a rematch," she said. "You picked the rocks, and my last one was a little off."

"That's interesting." His grin lit up his brown eyes, and the dark shadows she'd noted earlier weren't nearly so pronounced. "I didn't hear you complaining when you were ahead."

Charlotte shrugged. "Well, you obviously saved the defective rock for last."

"Me?" Dean asked in mock surprise. "I would never do something like that."

They started heading toward The Tidewater, but neither was in a huge hurry to return.

"As for your dad, don't sell him short," Charlotte said. "And don't give up on your mom yet."

"I won't. But I wish I wasn't so far away. If I could see for myself that she's all right, it would definitely put my mind at ease." He shook his head. "I've never been a patient man."

Charlotte gave a mock gasp. "Really?" She laughed, hoping to keep the mood light. He was doing so much better than when she'd first found him on the patio.

Dean laughed with her. "Yeah, I know. I need to work on it."

"Seriously, my offer to fill in for you at the restaurant still stands," she said. "I talked to Grace and Winnie. I hope you don't mind that I told them what was going on. Both are on board with me helping you out if you want to go to Florida."

"Charlotte—"

"And before you bring up the festival," she interrupted, "I talked to Pastor Abrams too. I didn't tell him about your mom. I only told him you've been very busy and could use some support with the talent show, and he promised to ask his nephew to lend a hand."

"I don't know what to say."

"'Thank you' will suffice," she told him.

"Thank you."

"You're welcome."

When they arrived at the patio, Dean stopped and turned to Charlotte. "Can you stay a little longer so we can go over everything?"

"Of course," she answered, following Dean into the restaurant. For the next hour, the two of them went over menus, specials, schedules, and back-up plans. By the time they were done, Charlotte was ready to take over The Tidewater's kitchen at the drop of a hat. But she hoped it didn't come down to that.

As Dean walked her to her car, he smiled. "All things considered, I had an oddly enjoyable time."

"You certainly know how to flatter a lady," Charlotte teased.

"No, I almost forgot how amazing you are in the kitchen. You had some great ideas for this week's menu. It was fun to brainstorm with someone else for a change. Thanks."

"My pleasure." She opened the car door and tossed her purse on the passenger seat. Then she faced him. "I'm praying that your mom gets good news, that at any moment now, the phone is going to ring and it'll be her saying it's a false alarm."

Dean nodded.

"However, if that doesn't happen," Charlotte continued, "I'm glad we have a plan in place so you can be there for her."

"Me too."

"And I want you to know that you're not alone," she said. "You have friends here you can lean on, who you can count on."

Dean smiled. "I'm a very lucky man."

As Charlotte drove home, she thought about what Dean had said. She had enjoyed her time with him too. Since working together at Le Crabe Fou, they'd definitely come a long way. They'd gone from bitter enemies to friends.

Eden

Eden was drowning in squares of fabric and patterns. The ladies in The Busy Bees—Winnie, Angel Diaz, Judith Mason, Patty Duncan, and Helen Daley—were buzzing around the room, talking, laughing, and exchanging stories and ideas. Eden had no idea where to start or what they were talking about. Her head began to spin, and Eden closed her eyes and counted to ten.

A cool hand settled on her forearm. "It's a bit overwhelming. But don't worry. We'll walk you through it."

She opened her eyes to meet Winnie's warm smile and Angel's knowing gaze.

"I think we should introduce you to some beginner patterns," Angel told Eden. "Maybe those cute reindeer place mats. Or that colorful runner and place mat set."

Winnie nodded.

"Oh, wait," Angel said. "I know what would be perfect for you. It's called a crazy quilt, and when I saw it earlier I thought of you. It would be a great beginner quilt."

"It does sound like my recent mood. I've certainly been feeling *stir*-crazy." Eden laughed and wondered how a woman she'd spent only five minutes with had figured her out so quickly.

Angel pulled up a website on her phone to show her a beautiful quilt that appeared way too advanced for her skill level, which was nonexistent.

"I love it," Eden said. "But I'm just starting out, so I should probably go with something easier and smaller."

"No, Angel's right," Winnie said. "And trust me. It's much easier than it looks, and you can call any mistakes part of the design, because the technique is all about seemingly random piecing. Plus, Judith has a bunch of scrap material. It's like it was meant to be."

The other women joined them, and they all agreed it would make a wonderful starter project for Eden.

Before Eden knew it, she had stacks of fat quarters—although she still wasn't sure what that meant—along with thin cotton-polyester batting, because it was apparently easy to work with. Not to mention needles, thread, shears, and the pattern.

Everyone had taken out their individual projects. As they worked, they talked Eden through the steps of piecing her quilt together.

"I understand you'll be here for our Holidaze Festival," Judith said to Eden. "You'll have to check out my husband's band."

"Your husband's in a band?" Eden asked.

Judith nodded. "He plays guitar in an oldies rock band. I call it his late midlife crisis."

The women laughed.

"It makes him happy," Judith continued. She paused in her work and grinned. "I'm fine with it as long as he doesn't come home with strange lipstick stains on his collar."

As the conversation flowed, Eden started getting to know the other women. They talked freely about themselves and their families and asked Eden questions about her life. Eden was surprised that the women seemed genuinely interested in her, even though they knew she was only passing through town.

"Winnie tells me you work in public relations," Patty said.

"Yes," Eden said. "I work for Bergman Relations in Atlanta."

"Do they handle actors?" Patty asked.

"We do represent several actors in our Los Angeles office," Eden said.

"Why do you ask?"

Patty beamed. "My son is going to need top-notch representation soon. Billy's very close to his big break."

"That's great," Eden said. "Is he working on anything right now?"

"Billy has an amazing role," Patty said, her eyes sparkling. "He's an alien on a brand-new science fiction show. It's going to be a huge hit."

"That's exciting news," Winnie said.

The others all chimed in with their congratulations and praise and asked questions about Billy's current project.

"Is he playing the title role?" Eden asked.

"No, but he could have been the lead," Patty replied. "Billy wanted a bigger challenge instead. His role has much more depth, and it will really stretch his acting skills."

"That's commendable," Eden said. "It sounds like he's planning ahead."

"Oh, he is," Patty said. "Billy's character is already a fan favorite, but he's going to be killed off in the fourth episode."

The rest of the women murmured their dismay.

Patty held up her hands. "No, it's fine. He says it's the ideal time because that's when the casting directors will be searching for actors for the new crop of shows."

"I wish Billy continued good luck," Eden said, then gave Patty the name and e-mail address of a colleague in their Los Angeles office for her son to reach out to for representation.

They worked for a few more hours, and Eden was surprised to see the quilt coming together. She was even more surprised to feel a sense of accomplishment and pride in what she had made so far. Never before had she thought of herself as a crafter. But she was learning that a hidden Eden lurked inside, and she liked this new person.

Her evening with the quilting group had made her realize

something else. Over the past few hours, Eden had bonded with these kind women. They had talked about their families and laughed together. The women were no longer strangers. They had become her friends.

Work had taken up so much of her time and energy over the years that Eden hadn't had a chance to form the kind of strong relationships these women had with each other.

And the fact that Eden had missed out on such meaningful friendships broke her heart.

10

Jenna

Jenna was nervous.

The feeling was silly as it wasn't her first date, although it was the first one in many months, and it was with Cole. Sweet, funny Cole. The guy she'd felt instantly at ease with when they'd met.

Hours earlier, she had been on the verge of calling Cole and begging off with some lame excuse. She'd asked the Magic 8-Ball if she should cancel the date. After giving the toy a good shake, she'd peeked at the answer.

My reply is no.

When it came to questions about Cole Briggs, she was beginning to believe the ball was rigged in his favor.

Now, as Jenna followed the hostess to their table overlooking Lake Haven, she chided herself for even thinking about backing out. Not only did she want to be on this date—something she didn't need a silly toy to tell her—but she needed it. It was normal to go on a date with a charming man, and her life needed to return to normal. Not that she'd had many charming men ask her out recently. In fact, her life had been sorely lacking in that department.

Her mother had always said that as soon as you stopped searching for something it would show up. Most of the time, her mother was right. As Jenna gazed across the table at her handsome date, it seemed like her mom had been spot-on once again.

Cole smiled and nodded toward the waitress.

Jenna could feel the heat rise in her cheeks as she realized the poor woman had been waiting on her to respond. "Oh, sorry. I was admiring the view."

"That's okay. It is breathtaking." The waitress rattled off The Tidewater's nightly specials and took their drink orders, then walked away.

"Are you enjoying your visit to Magnolia Harbor?" Cole asked.

"It's lovely," Jenna said with a sigh.

"That doesn't sound very encouraging."

What could she say? She didn't want to lie to Cole. That was a terrible way to start any relationship, even a friendship, and it was too early to burden him with all her family drama. "Are you kidding? I'm not sure I want to go home." Which was the truth.

"Don't you miss Charleston?" he asked.

Jenna shrugged. "I definitely don't miss the traffic."

"You've got a point there."

The waitress returned with their drinks, then took their orders.

After the waitress was gone, Cole said, "But Charleston has its perks. There's an amazing pub in the historic district. It's sort of hidden in the basement of a renovated mansion. Tours go through all day long, but they don't include the pub. To get to it, you have to go through an alley, just like the patrons did two hundred years ago."

Jenna smiled. "That sounds exactly like the kind of place my sister, Isobel, and I would love to visit."

"Maybe we can make it a double date some night," Cole said.

With his words, the weight of the world came slamming back on her shoulders. Isobel was dating an X-ray technician, and she would like nothing more than to hear her baby sister wanted to go on a double date. But then Jenna would have to come clean about her whereabouts. "Yeah, maybe."

The sadness she'd been drowning in all day must have seeped into her voice because Cole reached out and covered her hand with his. "It was only a suggestion, and if I misread the signs, then I apologize."

"No, it's a wonderful idea." Jenna covered her face with both hands and shook her head. *Stupid Magic 8-Ball.* She really should have canceled the date and stayed in for the night. The fight with Isobel had left her in a rotten mood, and now she'd hurt Cole's feelings. "I'm sorry. I had a bad day. Maybe we should do this another night."

"My uncle always says that talking about what's bothering you lightens the soul."

"That might be true," she said, "but you don't want to hear about my problems."

"Try me," Cole urged. "I promise I won't judge. I'll simply provide an ear to bend and a shoulder to cry on should you need one."

Jenna considered his kind offer, realizing it was probably the fastest and surest way to run him off, but she had to admit that she needed to talk to a friend right now.

The waitress delivered their meals, and for the next hour as they ate, Jenna told Cole everything. She explained how her sister had gotten the idea for them to take DNA tests so they could trace their family roots and how Jenna's results had informed her that she'd been adopted. She told him about her extended family driving her crazy and how she'd run away. Finally, she related her most recent phone call with Isobel.

Throughout the whole story, Cole did as he promised—he listened but didn't judge. He asked a question here or there to clarify, but not once did he say she overreacted or that she was ungrateful.

When Jenna finished, she asked, "So, are you wishing you'd had a buddy call with a fake emergency to get you out of this date?"

"No," Cole said. "I'm thinking that you've had a rough couple of months and you certainly deserve the chocolate cake on the dessert menu."

Was Cole for real, or was she dreaming? She'd heard stories about men like him—genuine, kind, and caring—but she'd given up hope on finding one.

"The chocolate cake sounds great, but you have to share it with me," she said.

He smiled. "It's a deal."

After they put in the dessert order with the waitress, Jenna gazed out the window. Lake Haven was beautiful, and the moon was playing peekaboo with the clouds overhead. But the evening had turned too chilly to go walking along the water's edge, so they'd have to enjoy the view from inside.

"Thank you for hearing me out," Jenna said as she faced Cole. "You're a good listener. You must take after your uncle."

"Actually, Glen isn't my uncle by blood," he replied. "He's my stepfather's brother."

Shocked by his revelation, she sat back in her chair. When she had watched Cole's interactions with the pastor, she'd assumed that they were not only blood relations but a very tight-knit family.

"My parents divorced when I was still a baby," Cole explained. "Then my mom met Roger, and they married when I was five. As far as I'm concerned, Roger is my dad. He was there to teach me how to ride my bike, and he was the one who picked me up when I fell off it and broke my arm. He helped me with math and read my essay papers and taught me how to drive a car. He was there for a lot more than that, but you get what I'm saying."

"I do," Jenna said.

"Any guy can be a father—"

"But it takes a special man to be a dad," she finished for him.

"Exactly. The guy whose name is on my birth certificate served his purpose. From what I've heard and learned over the years, I'm much better off for him stepping aside and letting Roger raise me."

"I feel that way about my parents too," Jenna admitted. "I love them, and even if I'm mad at them, I don't want to trade them in."

"You'd probably get a good deal," he joked.

"True, especially if my mom gave out samples of her cooking."

Cole grinned.

The waitress breezed over and set a piece of chocolate cake in the middle of the table along with napkins and two forks. "Enjoy," she said, then walked away.

Cole pushed the dessert plate toward Jenna, letting her go first. "What's the best thing your mom makes?"

The question conjured up so many wonderful memories of holidays, birthdays, Sunday dinners, and even elaborate tea parties. Memories of the family gathered together, laughing, talking, eating, and sharing their lives. Beautiful moments worth remembering because of her mother who got them all together and knew how to bring out the best in everyone.

"I can't name just one thing," Jenna said. "My mom's the best cook you'd ever meet. Well, unless you want a grilled cheese sandwich. If you ask for one, you're either going to get two lovely pieces of toast with cold cheese in the middle or a blackened mess of goo."

"Anyone can make grilled cheese sandwiches."

"Not my mom. But she can make anything else."

"Jambalaya?" Cole asked.

Jenna snorted. "In her sleep."

"Shrimp étouffée?"

"The best in three counties." She knew her voice carried a hint of pride, but her mom's cooking deserved it. "I'm telling you, she can cook anything but grilled cheese. If you asked for a sandwich, she'd try. It would be made with love, but it wouldn't be edible."

"My mom's the opposite," Cole said. "She can grill a sandwich but not a whole lot else. She leaves the cooking to Roger. Thankfully, he knows his way around a kitchen. And while he's cooking up the best beef stew, he's usually fixing something around the house."

"Sounds like my dad. He likes to putter around. He's always fixing something."

"Your parents sound pretty amazing," Cole said.

Jenna knew they were, and she didn't need Cole or anyone else to point that out to her, although it was nice to hear it from an outsider. While she was growing up and listening to her classmates' complaints about their parents, Jenna was fully aware that she'd won the parental lottery. They weren't overtly strict. But there were rules and consequences when those rules weren't followed.

The best thing about Jenna's mom and dad was the fact that they were always there for her and Isobel. Her parents were ready to listen, and while they did offer advice, they didn't attempt to rule their daughters' lives and dictate their every step. Both girls were allowed to make their own mistakes. When Jenna and Isobel fell down, their parents picked them up, dusted them off, and encouraged them to try again.

Unable to eat another bite of the decadent chocolate cake, Jenna pushed the plate toward Cole. "They're incredible, which is why I can't trade them. I mean, I've got them trained almost perfectly at this point. Could you imagine starting over?"

"No way. It would take so much work to build that relationship," Cole said. "Do you have any desire to meet your biological family?"

"Absolutely not," she said. "The website we took the DNA test through has sent me a few e-mails about potential family members. Some of them look like pretty close relatives. I'm sure they're wonderful people, but that's not fair to my birth parents or my real parents."

"Why do you say that?" Cole asked, his voice softening. It was obvious that he really wanted to know the answer and wasn't asking simply to make polite conversation.

"My birth parents had their reasons for giving me up. I respect whatever those reasons were. And they've been living all this time without me. They don't deserve to have their lives disrupted now because I took a test. What if they got remarried or had more kids and never told anyone about me? Then I'd be upsetting more people's lives. I know what it feels like, and I wouldn't want to do that to someone else."

"I can understand that logic. Besides, you never know what you're getting yourself into." He raised his brows. "They might all be crazy. Or criminals. Or spies."

"I can deal with crazy. My family doesn't hide our crazy relatives. We park them on the porch in a rocker." Jenna grinned. "At least that's where Aunt Lenore will be during our next gathering."

Cole chuckled. "Yeah, I know what you mean. I have a great-uncle like that too."

They finished their dessert, and Cole suggested they order coffee and take their cups outside to the patio, where there were several heaters and a couple of firepits. Jenna wasn't ready for the night to end, so she quickly agreed.

When they took their coffee out to the patio and sat down, Cole started telling her amusing stories about his childhood.

Soon Jenna forgot all about her argument with her sister. For the first time in days, the stress and worries of the past couple of months didn't weigh heavily on her shoulders. Jenna allowed herself to enjoy the rest of the night and Cole's company.

On the drive back to the inn, Jenna reflected on the wonderful evening she'd had. There had been much laughter but so much more. Cole put her at ease. There was a connection between them that just happened. She didn't have to try to make it work. It was effortless.

When Cole walked her up the steps of the inn, he took her hand. "Jenna Salzman, woman of mystery, I'd really like to see you again. Will you go to the dance with me on Friday?"

She smiled and batted her eyelashes playfully. "Well, I don't have my trusty Magic 8-Ball handy to consult. So I'm going to have to wing it and say . . . yes."

11

Eden

"Good morning," Eden said as she entered the kitchen. "My goodness. Did I oversleep?"

Charlotte pulled eggs, vegetables, and seasonings out of the large refrigerator, and Grace and Winnie sat at the marble-topped island sipping coffee.

"No, you're right on time," Charlotte answered. "We're going to make a rainbow frittata for breakfast. And I thought you might like to prepare the hors d'oeuvres for this evening's social hour with me."

"Would you like a cup of decaf coffee?" Grace asked.

"Yes, please," Eden said.

Grace went over to the coffeepot on the counter and poured a cup. As she handed it to Eden, she said, "Winnie was telling us about the quilt you're making. I hope you brought it down to show us."

"It's right here." Eden held up the bag she'd purchased to store her project and sewing supplies in. She set the bag on the island, then carefully removed the quilt in progress and put it on the counter.

Charlotte stopped her prep work to peer over Grace's shoulder. "Oh, I love that deep purple. It's so vibrant and regal."

"It's a beautiful pattern," Grace remarked. "Winnie, I'm officially putting this quilt on my Christmas wish list, maybe with some blues in it."

"Yes ma'am," Winnie said with a laugh. "At the rate Eden's going, she might be able to finish a second quilt before the week's out. She's a natural." She gestured at the quilt. "Look at this stitching. It's perfect."

"You're too kind," Eden said, then took a sip of her coffee. "Honestly, I probably stabbed my thumb a good dozen or more times."

In spite of her sore thumb, Eden had enjoyed her evening with the quilting group. The camaraderie she'd discovered with the other women had left her relaxed, recharged, and ready to take on the world, but she'd also thoroughly enjoyed the process of quilting. It took focus and skill—not that she had a lot at this stage—and patience. It kept her mind and body busy without overtaxing it, which should make her doctor and her heart very happy.

Eden folded the quilt and packed it away in her bag before washing her hands and saluting to Charlotte. "Okay, master, I'm ready to learn. Where do I start today?"

"I could get used to that title," Charlotte said with a grin.

Grace rolled her eyes. "Please don't encourage her ego."

Winnie chuckled, clearly used to the gentle teasing between the two sisters.

Eden imagined moments like this must remind Winnie of her older sister, Grace and Charlotte's late mother, Hazel, about whom she'd heard lovely things. While that loss would be heartbreaking, at least being with her nieces would be like having a piece of her sister still with her.

Charlotte handed Eden a knife and the vegetables. "I need you to cube the sweet potatoes into half-inch chunks, the sweet yellow peppers about the same, and then coarsely chop the broccoli."

"All of this is going in our breakfast?" Eden asked as she eyed the colorful mix in front of her.

Charlotte nodded. "We're going to eat the rainbow and start your day on a healthy note."

"All right," Eden replied, trying to sound like she was on board. But she found broccoli for breakfast unappetizing and sweet potatoes without cinnamon and brown sugar boring. She suppressed a sigh and started chopping.

Eden chided herself for being dramatic. So far, nothing Charlotte had cooked had been boring or tasteless. Surely this healthy breakfast wouldn't let her down either.

While Eden chopped vegetables, the sisters discussed the upcoming festival with their aunt.

"Are either of you girls going to the dance?" Winnie asked.

"I'm not sure," Grace said.

"It depends on if Dean has to fly to Florida or not," Charlotte said. "If he does, I'll probably be working at The Tidewater."

"What about you?" Winnie asked Eden. "Will you be going to the dance?"

Eden turned from the counter where she'd been working. All the vegetables were cut and stacked in neat little piles. "I'm not sure. It sounds like a lot of fun, but dancing might be more than I'm ready for. Besides, I don't have a date."

"We can enjoy the music together," Winnie suggested. "The quilting group will be there too. So you won't be alone."

Warmth and a sense of belonging spread throughout Eden with Winnie's kind words. "Thank you. In that case, I can't wait for the dance." She frowned. "Except I don't have anything to wear. Maybe I can talk Jenna into going shopping with me."

"That sounds like a wonderful idea," Grace said. "I can give you a couple of recommendations for places nearby." She picked up a notepad and jotted down a list of local shops, then gave the piece of paper to Eden.

"Thank you," Eden said, scanning the list.

"Miss Millie's on Main Street is terrific," Grace said as she placed her coffee cup in the dishwasher. "I'd better get started on my chores."

Before Grace could leave the kitchen, excited barking outside drew all their attention.

Eden peeked out the window to see Winston and a chocolate Lab racing around in circles.

Spencer, the neighbor Eden had met earlier in the week, walked into the kitchen. "Good morning, ladies." He greeted them all, but his focus was on Grace.

They returned his greeting, and Charlotte joined Eden at the counter to walk her through the recipe.

"What brings you by this morning, Spencer?" Grace smiled, and Eden thought there was something special in the expression.

"Enjoying the nice weather while it lasts," he said. "Bailey and I were taking an early walk, and we thought we'd see if you and Winston would like to join us."

Grace gazed wistfully out the large window to the sunny day beyond and then back to her sister and aunt, her smile fading. "That's sweet of you to think of us, but I've got a lot to do around here—"

"Nonsense," Winnie interrupted. "Charlotte and I can handle anything urgent, and the rest can wait."

It was pretty clear to Eden where Grace's heart lay, and it wasn't the weather that tempted her to abandon her responsibilities.

Of course, if Eden had the attention of a man like Spencer, she'd be tempted too. From what she'd seen and heard, Spencer was kind, patient, helpful, and upstanding. While he was friendly to all of them, it was clear he only had eyes for Grace. Not that it appeared either of them was aware of what rested beneath their friendship, and it wasn't Eden's business to point it out either. She was a public relations professional, not a matchmaker.

"Go on." Charlotte waved her sister toward the door. "Take advantage and enjoy the morning out."

"If you're waffling between making my bed or taking a handsome man up on his offer, I'm going to worry about you," Eden chimed in. Okay, she couldn't help sticking her nose in a little bit.

"I think they're trying to get rid of you," Spencer said with a grin. "It's not your birthday, is it?"

"No, it's not." Grace threw up her hands and laughed. "But it does sound like I'm outvoted. Let me grab my hat and Winston's leash."

After they left the kitchen, Winnie said, "While you two get breakfast made, I'll freshen up the rooms. I'm feeling a tad restless this morning."

Charlotte's hands stilled, and she eyed her aunt critically. "Are you okay?"

Winnie patted Charlotte's shoulder and chuckled. "I'm fine. It's probably the slice of sweet potato pie I had last night. I couldn't help myself." Then she told Eden, "I have diabetes, and I need to watch my sugar."

Eden nodded. So she wasn't the only one who had a restrictive diet.

When Winnie went upstairs, Eden and Charlotte got down to the business of cooking—sautéing vegetables, mixing, measuring, and finally sliding the rainbow frittata into the oven.

"Let's take a coffee break before tackling the appetizers," Charlotte suggested.

As they sat at the island to enjoy a second cup of coffee, Eden glanced upward. "You're so lucky to have an aunt. Winnie's been fabulous to me this week. You and Grace have too. I feel like I'm visiting family, not staying at an inn."

Charlotte blew on her coffee before responding. "Thank you. That's probably one of the best compliments anyone can ever give us. Getting to know our guests is one of my favorite things about running a bed-and-breakfast. And honestly, you and Jenna have become more than guests to us."

"I can't wait to come back. I'm not sure I even want to leave Magnolia Harbor."

"It does grow on you, but wouldn't you miss your family?" Charlotte got up to take a peek in the oven and refresh their coffee cups.

"It's only me," Eden said. "My parents are gone, and I don't have any siblings. I was married a long time ago, but my work habits destroyed that. In retrospect, I can't say I blame him for ending things. It couldn't have been much fun being alone in a marriage."

"I'm so sorry to hear that," Charlotte said.

"Over the years, I've given a lot of advice to my clients," Eden said. She shook her head. "I should have taken some of it myself."

"What would you have done differently?" Charlotte asked.

"I would have put my marriage before my career," Eden admitted. "When you find the one to settle down with, please don't make the same mistake."

12

Charlotte

After finishing the cooking lesson with Eden and serving breakfast, Charlotte returned to her small cottage located on the inn's property. As soon as she walked through the door, she received a call from Dean.

"Can you come over?" Dean asked. He sounded out of breath. "I need your help."

"Of course," she said without hesitating. "I'll be right there."

Charlotte twisted up her long hair, applied the barest minimum of makeup, and donned a pair of black twill pants and a lightweight cotton shirt that would be comfortable under a chef's jacket. She didn't know exactly what Dean needed, but with the versatile outfit, she was ready for whatever came her way.

Arriving at The Tidewater, she spotted a tour bus in the parking lot, so she wasn't surprised when the receptionist directed her to the kitchen.

Weaving through a full dining room, she smiled at the guests and waitstaff, trying to guess what waited for her behind the closed doors ahead. All was calm, and it appeared to be business as usual out front. Perhaps Dean had resolved his issue already.

She stepped into the kitchen. It was too quiet. Where was the '80s music Dean was so fond of playing in the background while he prepped for a meal?

Charlotte stopped and took in the scene before her. With the exception of the somber atmosphere, it didn't seem too bad. The staff members were diligently working at their stations. Vegetables were being chopped. The sweet smell of melting butter sizzled in the air. Dishes clanged in the sink.

Then her gaze landed on Dean, and she did a double take.

He stood staring at a saucepan, spoon suspended in midair. Something that resembled oatmeal fell off the spoon and landed in the pan. She wasn't sure what to call the stuff. It didn't look like any sauce she'd ever seen before.

After dropping off her purse in the office, Charlotte grabbed a spare chef's jacket and made her way around the kitchen, saying hello to everyone. When she reached Dean, she peered into the pan. The lumpy contents were not quite cream colored but sort of a greenish yellow. "What have you got there? Is that a lemon-lime glaze, or are you getting a head start on St. Patrick's Day with green oatmeal?"

Dean shook his head and laughed. "Not even close. It's hollandaise."

"Oh . . . wow." Charlotte tilted her head. "Why is it green?"

"I might have put basil in it," he replied. "Or maybe it was dill."

"But that doesn't—"

"I know that neither of those belong in a hollandaise sauce," Dean interrupted. "But I seem to have forgotten how to make even the most basic of sauces." He stared at her, and his eyes were filled with pain, fear, and frustration.

She'd never seen Dean mess up a dish before. They'd worked through some pretty intense situations at Le Crabe Fou—holidays, nights with half the staff out sick, critics in the house—and Dean had never lost his cool. He had never slipped up in the kitchen and missed one single ingredient, burned a dished, or undercooked an entrée. When it came to cooking, Dean Bradley was an artist. He created culinary masterpieces because everything he made came from a place of love. Cooking was his passion.

It was time to put him back in touch with his muse.

"You have a restaurant full of guests, and I'm sure they would love to meet the chef," Charlotte said. "Why don't you go schmooze with them while I handle this?"

Dean studied the goopy mess in the pan, then reached up and rubbed the back of his neck. "Are you sure?"

She nodded. "Go sprinkle some of that famous charm in the dining room, and I'll work my magic to turn this into something edible."

"How do you plan to do that?" he asked.

"I'm going to dump it in the trash and start over." Charlotte tried to keep a straight face but ended up grinning at him. Honestly, there was no saving that sauce.

Dean laughed, which was her goal, and walked out.

Charlotte threw out the sauce, then switched on the radio, which had the desired effect on the kitchen crew. Within minutes, the heavy mood in the room lifted and the staff was talking and working in sync as orders came in and dishes went out.

She took a moment to peer out the door to check on Dean and saw him laughing with a group of elderly ladies who were clearly flirting with him. Not that his ego needed the boost, but she was glad to see some of the old Dean return.

By the time Dean finished making his rounds of the dining room and returned to the kitchen, Charlotte had everything under control. She shooed him out to talk to the new diners and handle the paperwork in his office.

Once the lunch rush was over, she found him sitting at his desk staring at a picture on the wall.

It was a family photo taken at Christmas. Given it had Dean, his parents, and his brother, sister-in-law, and their kids as well, she guessed it had been taken on a timer. What she loved most about the picture was the fact that it wasn't perfect. Or maybe it was because no one was looking at the camera. The twin boys were making faces at each other. Dean was laughing with his brother and sister-in-law, and his parents were smiling at the whole family. In other words, it was a treasured moment.

"Looks like you and your family had a great time that day," Charlotte remarked, gesturing at the photo.

"We did. It was last Christmas. We haven't all been together since then." Dean pushed his chair back, ran his hands through his hair, and glanced around his office before reaching for the door. "Let's take a walk."

Charlotte didn't question him. Dean reminded her of a caged animal, except he was trapped in a moment of life and there was no escape. There was only patience and prayer.

They exited through the front doors and headed away from the inn. Then they walked down a different set of trails along the lake through the bare trees until they came to a spot that had been cleared.

A couple of stumps remained, and Charlotte and Dean sat down on them. They had a great view of Lake Haven.

They remained silent for a few moments, letting the calming sounds of nature fill the void.

"Thanks for coming to my rescue today," Dean said.

"You don't have to thank me."

"This is the second time you've rescued me," he added.

"Oh, you're right," Charlotte said. "In that case, you're welcome. If you're going to make a habit out of this, I might have to come up with a superhero name for myself. Maybe even get a cape."

Dean laughed. "Yeah, that sauce was pretty bad."

"It was like green oatmeal," she teased.

For a moment, she thought he was going to snap at her. But then peals of laughter exploded from Dean until tears ran down his cheeks.

"Maybe I should install some kind of emergency signal when I need your help. I could turn it on, and a giant skillet and crossed knives would light up the sky over the inn."

Charlotte shook her head. "That reminds me of a pirate. It might freak out my guests."

"How about a red phone with a special ringtone?" he suggested.

"What if I'm away from the inn?"

"Good point. Maybe a special ringtone on your phone instead."

"Do I dare ask what it would be?"

"That's easy," Dean said. "'Holding Out for a Hero.'"

Heat exploded across her cheeks, and she ducked her head so Dean couldn't see her embarrassment. Charlotte didn't feel like a hero. She hadn't done anything beyond what anyone else would have done for a friend.

"Okay, for once your obsession with '80s music has paid off as that's a good choice," Charlotte said. "But I have a feeling you won't be needing me to come to your rescue very often."

Dean sighed. "If things keep going the way they have been, I might need to take you up on your other offer of filling in for me at the restaurant."

"What happened?" she asked softly.

There was that pain and frustration she'd seen earlier in his eyes. "Marc called this morning. He told me the 'little test' Mom had was actually surgery."

Charlotte gasped. "But that's good news, right? Because you've talked to her and she's home and doing well?"

"Yes and no," Dean said. "She is doing well, and I'm grateful for that. What I don't like is that I thought they were doing a simple biopsy, but they removed the tumor and the surrounding tissue. She was in the hospital for a couple of days and didn't even tell us anything until after the fact."

"Did your mom say why?"

"No, she isn't aware that I know the truth yet. Or maybe by now, Marc has confessed to her that he told me. But either way, I wish I'd heard it from her. I'm sure she didn't want us to worry, but I'm an adult. I can handle my feelings about the truth, and I would have walked through this with her."

"Parents are always trying to protect their children, no matter how old they are," Charlotte said.

"Yeah, sometimes I think she still sees Marc and me as little boys."

"I think it's more than that. Obviously, I don't have kids, but as an aunt I see what Grace goes through with Jake. It's not so much that she still sees that little boy. She's so proud of the young man he's grown up to be, but she can't help her innate need to guide and protect him. It's the mom gene. I'm betting that's all your mom was doing too."

Dean shrugged and dropped his gaze. "Maybe. But there's more."

"Tell me," Charlotte urged.

"According to Marc, Mom got her results back, but the doctors are stumped. They've forwarded the samples to Yale oncology."

"I'm glad. I mean, Yale is one of the best, and if anyone can figure out what is going on with your mom, they can. Did Marc say how long until you hear the results?"

"They're expecting them within a few more days." He avoided her eyes, pain etched deep in his face. "I'm scared. What if they can't figure out what's wrong with her?"

How could Charlotte tell him to prepare for the worst, pray for the best, and treasure every minute he had with his mom? She couldn't take away his hope, and deep down she believed there was still a chance. "Let's not lose faith yet. Modern medicine is pretty amazing, and don't forget your mom's strong will. It's okay to be scared, but I do think you need to let go of your anger."

"Maybe I don't want to," Dean muttered.

"I understand you're hurt and angry that your mom and dad didn't tell you everything, and I know it's easier to focus on that than how afraid you are," she said gently. "However, as much as we might not like it, they don't have to. It's their decision. Not ours."

"But I'm their son," he protested.

"I'm not saying it doesn't affect you," Charlotte went on. "I'm only saying it's not your decision on how to handle the situation. And maybe your parents are scared too and don't want you and Marc to see their fear."

Dean snorted in disbelief. He got up and marched to the edge of the lake, where he leaned against a bare oak tree. "My mom and dad have never been afraid of anything in their lives."

"You might be surprised at how wrong that statement is."

He whirled around and stared at her. "What do you mean?"

"All parents are afraid at one point or another." Charlotte pushed off the stump and joined him. "Think about some of the dumb things we did as kids and as teens. Now tell me you never struck fear into your parents. I know I sure did. My poor mom used to clutch the dashboard and pray for her life when I was learning to drive."

"That's different," Dean said. "That's not real fear."

"Oh, trust me. That was real. I was an awful driver." She paused for dramatic effect. "I may have even hit a cow once."

His eyes went wide, and then he smirked. "A cow? Well, they are kind of small and hard to see. Plus, they move so fast. They tend to dart out right in front of you. I can understand how you could hit one."

They both laughed, and the tension that had built between them dissipated.

Charlotte knew that she would regret sharing that tidbit with him in the future, but for now it was worth it.

"You know, for a person who hit a cow, you're pretty smart," Dean said.

She elbowed him in the ribs. Apparently the hypothetical future had been a lot sooner than she'd thought. "Thanks."

"I understand what you're saying. I don't like it, but you're right. It's my mom's life, and I have to respect her decisions."

They fell into a companionable silence for a few moments.

Charlotte glanced around the clearing again. They were still on land owned by Dean and The Tidewater's other investor. "What's with the clearing? Are you expanding the inn?"

"We're going to build a gazebo so guests can come down here to read and relax," he answered. "We could also reserve it for anniversaries or even small weddings. Nothing elaborate or on the scale that you and Grace offer. It'll be just another service to complement our business."

"It's an ideal location and a great idea." Charlotte would have to scratch that item off her list of suggestions. She wouldn't want Dean to think she was copying him. She would refer anyone searching for a gazebo ceremony to The Tidewater. After all, Charlotte and Grace were staying plenty busy these days. "I probably should get back to the inn. I left Grace alone to do the work."

"I'll walk you to your car," Dean offered.

When they reached her Camry, Dean drew her in and gave her a long hug. "Thank you."

"Yeah, yeah. I'm amazing." She brushed off his thanks, feeling uncomfortable and not really wanting to go but unsure why. So she handled it the best she knew how when it came to Dean and laughed about it.

"All kidding aside, I don't know how I would have gotten through the last few days without you," Dean admitted.

"You're welcome," she said. "If you need me again, let it ring three times, hang up, and then call back and let it ring three more times. That'll be our special chef-in-distress code."

"Sure thing," Dean said, his face brightening. Then he walked away, leaving Charlotte with all kinds of feelings she didn't want to examine.

Jenna

"Good boy," Jenna said, giving Winston a treat. She'd been working with him on his tricks of waving hello, spinning in a circle, and taking a bow. The adorable dog was doing a great job on all of them.

Winston gobbled up the treat and wagged his tail.

She smiled and patted his furry head. "You're a shoo-in for the blue ribbon at the dog show."

Winston yipped.

"It looks like Winston is making good progress," Eden said, walking over to them.

"He sure is," Jenna said. "By the way, breakfast was delicious."

"I hope this evening's appetizers turn out well too," Eden said. "I helped Charlotte with them."

"Can't wait to try them," Jenna said.

The women talked for a few minutes about their upcoming plans and the festival that was set to begin that evening.

"Are you free to go shopping tomorrow?" Eden asked. "Although I don't have anyone to impress, I'd rather not show up at the dance in jeans or business casual clothes, which is all I have with me."

"I'd love to." Jenna glanced down at her soft flannel shirt, well-worn jeans, and sneakers. It was a far cry from what she had in mind for the dance. "I didn't bring anything suitable to wear either." She felt her cheeks flush. "And I have a date with Cole."

"That's wonderful," Eden said, smiling. "Grace gave me a list of stores in the area. She said the one on Main Street called Miss Millie's is terrific."

"Sounds good," Jenna said, then checked the time on her phone. "I'm sorry, but I'd better get going. I promised Pastor Abrams that I would help him set up the kids' games at the festival."

"Of course," Eden said. "Let's plan to meet after lunch tomorrow."

Jenna agreed, then returned to the inn with Winston at her heels.

After retrieving her purse and keys from her room, Jenna jumped into her car and drove to Magnolia Harbor. The waterfront park was bustling. Half the town must have been there to get ready for that evening's kickoff of the Holidaze Festival.

Jenna sidestepped piles of wood, buckets, and boxes as she searched for Glen. She thought of her current activities and chuckled. Most people wouldn't consider training a dog and volunteering at the local church much of a vacation, but she was relishing every minute of it.

Spotting the pastor's wild hair, Jenna waved and tried not to freak out at the number of spots marked with a giant X. While she was glad to lend a hand, she also wanted some time for herself. Maybe she could get a facial and a manicure after she went shopping with Eden.

"I'm glad you could make it." Glen smiled and shook her hand. "How good are you with a hammer?"

Before Jenna could answer his question, her phone rang. She knew that ringtone. It was Isobel. Jenna grabbed her phone and quickly hit the decline option, then slipped her phone into her back pocket. "Pretty good. My dad made sure my sister and I learned how to hit the nail and not our thumbs."

The pastor smiled. "That's good because I always hit my thumb." He pointed out various locations and the truck parked along the curb. "These are all reserved for the game booths."

Thankfully, there were only five. It was less than Jenna had originally estimated.

"The rest are booths reserved by individuals and businesses, both local and out of town," he said.

"I thought this was a church event," she said.

Glen signaled her to follow him as he headed toward the truck, where they started unloading equipment and supplies. "The Fellowship Christian Church is sponsoring the Holidaze Festival to raise money for our local food bank."

"This seems a lot bigger than what most churches put on."

"It certainly is," he said. "It started out as a one-day event. But when word got out, the town rallied behind it, and now the festival is scheduled to last a little over four days."

"It's wonderful that the town is so supportive," Jenna remarked. "Will the food bank get all the profits?"

"The rental fees from the booths all go to the food bank," Glen answered. "The profits stay with the businesses, or they can donate a portion. It's up to each. We've set up a donation box so people can give money anonymously and not worry about judgment. We know there are people who don't have the luxury to give."

"But in a way, you're helping out more than just the food bank," Jenna observed.

Once again, her phone rang. Ignoring it, she smiled at the pastor and grabbed a couple of boxes.

He hefted a load of wood onto his shoulders. "We're helping others to help themselves, and that's the best thing we can do. Hopefully, we'll have a great turnout like we did in the spring for the Strawberry Festival. The success of that event was why the town wanted to expand this festival into something bigger. We had a lot of out-of-town traffic that was good for the local businesses."

They set down their first load, and her phone rang again.

"Do you need to get that?" he asked.

"No, it's only my sister," she replied. "Where do we start?"

The two of them went to work on the first booth. Kids would throw beanbags at a line of balloons. If they hit a balloon, it would press against a tack and pop, eliminating the possibility of a passerby getting hit by a stray dart. Jenna thought whoever had come up with the idea was a genius as she could remember a few stray darts in her youth.

First, they put together what resembled a bookshelf with an open back. Then Jenna nailed a thin wooden strip across the middle of each shelf. Next, she glued tacks every six inches across the wooden strip. While she applied the finishing touches to the first game, Glen brought more supplies from the truck to their stations.

Once again, her phone rang as he walked by, and once again, Jenna ignored it. She was tempted to turn off her phone, but what if Cole called?

The pastor set down the last load before reaching into a cooler she hadn't noticed before and handing her a bottle of water. "That's a mighty fine balloon-popping thingy." He laughed and shook his head. "Sorry, but I'm not exactly sure what you call it without the darts. It's not really a dartboard now, is it?"

It seemed like everything around Jenna was changing, even children's games. Nothing was safe. Nothing was sacred. Maybe that was what bothered her the most. If something like her family could be ripped away, if something she had always counted on to be there, to be true, could be proven false, then what else could she be wrong about? The very thought chilled her to her bones.

Jenna pressed the cool bottle against the back of her neck, surprised to find she'd worked up a bit of a sweat. "Do you think that will bother the kids? The game being different than what they're used to?"

Glen studied the booth and smiled. "No, I don't think they'll even notice the difference for more than a few seconds. They'll most likely focus on what they know, accept the changes, and move on. Most kids are pretty adaptable."

"Unlike adults?"

"We do get set in our ways as we get older," he said. "We become creatures of habit and worry that change is going to crack our foundations and make the world crumble around us, instead of opening new pathways for us to explore."

"What if you don't want to go down a new pathway?" she asked.

Jenna had no intention of going down any pathway that might lead to a new family. Goodness only knew what she'd discover if she did. The family she had might not be perfect, but she knew them and loved them, even if they drove her crazy sometimes.

A new thought hit her, and it frightened her even more than all the other thoughts she'd had since this whole revelation had come to light. What if doing the DNA test led her biological family to her? What if they came searching for her? She had no plans to look for them, but what if they showed up on her doorstep?

What a tangled web of a nightmare she'd unwittingly walked into.

"Is that what the avoided phone calls are about?" Glen asked.

Lost in thought, Jenna had forgotten her own question and had to rack her brain to remember what she'd asked. It was easier to start at the beginning, so she told him the whole story.

He mulled over her words and scratched his head, making his hair stand up even more than before, causing Jenna to bite back a laugh.

"Thanks for sharing your story with me," the pastor said, his voice low and soothing. "I could tell something has been weighing heavily on your mind. It sounds like you love your family very much and they love you just as much."

"I've never really doubted that they love me, but how could they lie to me for so long?" Jenna asked. "My parents always stressed the importance of honesty above all else. I thought we were so close."

"Yet you admitted you lied to them and your sister about where you are this week," Glen reminded her.

She sat down on the grass and groaned. "I know I have no right to toss that stone considering I'm living in a glass house."

He sat next to her. "Maybe you should give yourself and your family a break. No one is perfect. Parenting isn't easy. Sadly, kids don't come with a manual, probably because it would have to be rewritten for each one. I think your parents did what they felt in their hearts was the best thing for you, your sister, and them."

Jenna started to object, but she didn't know what to say anymore, having lost the steam of her argument as his words settled around her.

"All families are messy and complicated, even mine," Glen continued. "There's no such thing as the perfect family. That's a fairy tale made up in Hollywood. But what's just as important as the family you are given is the family you create and the love you share."

Jenna considered his comments as they set up the next game station. She thought of her parents and sister. Then she remembered being at friends' houses growing up and gaining stolen insights into their lives.

Thankfully, no one she knew had an awful life, but it wasn't always sunshine and rainbows either. Some of her friends' parents fought or could be extremely demanding or overly critical. Another had a dad who had to travel a lot for work and missed out on important events. When it came to the parental lottery, Jenna had really hit the jackpot.

She decided to call her parents on Sunday after the family gathering was over. She'd explain why she was upset and reassure them that she loved them.

Glen touched her arm with his phone in his other hand. "I need to run to the church and handle an issue that's come up. Can you take care of this last station? It's an inflatable basketball hoop. I'll get someone over here as soon as I can to clean the area, so don't worry about any of that."

"I've got it covered," Jenna assured him. "You go take care of business."

"Thank you," he said and hurried away.

Before Jenna started putting together the last game station, she texted her sister. *Is there a family emergency?*

After a few minutes, Isobel responded. *No.*

Okay. I'm busy right now, but I'll call you later. I promise. Jenna pocketed the phone.

The inflatable basketball hoop was bigger than she expected and much heavier. Struggling to get it out of the box, she ended up leaning backward and heaving with all her might. The hoop popped loose, and Jenna landed on her backside, staring at the blue sky. She was glad no one saw her fall.

Or at least she thought no one saw until she heard a deep chuckle and gazed up into a pair of blue eyes the same shade as the summer sky.

"Need a hand?" Cole asked.

Jenna couldn't believe that Cole of all people had seen her embarrassing display. "I'm good."

"So you're taking a break?" he teased.

"Well, I am on vacation," Jenna replied. She could stay here forever and stare at his gorgeous eyes and charming smile. The combination chased away the blues and made her forget about the issues going on at home.

"I have a better idea," Cole said as he helped her stand. "How about we finish setting this up together and then get some ice cream?"

"It's a little cold for ice cream."

"Says the woman who was just lying on the ground."

Jenna laughed. "Good point."

Together they stretched out the rubber basketball game, positioned it over the giant *X*, and hammered the stakes into the ground to keep it from flying off to Kansas with the first good wind.

As they worked, Cole talked about the unusual day he'd had so far. He'd rescued a kitten from a tree, a client's sprinkler system had switched on unexpectedly and soaked him from head to toe, and then he'd landed a huge contract.

"All that and the day's not even over," she said.

He smiled. "Let's not forget to add rescuing a damsel in distress to my list of accomplishments."

Jenna grinned and fired up the air compressor. "I'd hardly call that a rescue or say I was in distress. But you did help me with this monstrosity, which probably weighs almost as much as I do. And you promised me ice cream, so you get points for being a true Southern gentleman."

Cole turned off the compressor and sealed the inflatable basketball hoop before picking up one of the basketballs out of a nearby box. "You seem to be in a better mood."

"What do you mean?" Jenna asked. Maybe he was referring to their dinner the night before. She had been off her game and not really in the mood for a date. But she thought they'd ended the evening on a high note when he had asked her to go to the dance with him.

He bounced the ball and glanced away as if hesitant to share his thoughts with her. "It's nothing. Just something my uncle said."

Jenna took a step back. Her hand automatically shot to her stomach, which was suddenly a riot of nerves. Cole knew the DNA and adoption story, but had she told the pastor anything else? She hadn't expected Glen to share her confidences with others, not even Cole.

Her thoughts must have shown on her face because Cole told her, "He only said he was worried about you. That you were carrying a weight."

"Oh." She grabbed a fresh bottle of water and drained half of it in one go. "Sorry. I wasn't implying that he would break a trust. I guess I didn't realize you two talk so often. You seem very close."

"We are. Uncle Glen has been there for me since I was a kid. He's always loved and accepted me, even though we're not related by blood, like my stepdad. Family is all about love, and it doesn't have anything to do with DNA—that's science."

Jenna nodded. "I know what you mean. My family has been the same. And they've always supported me no matter what."

He handed her the basketball. "We need to make sure the ball can take a beating. We can't have it losing air right in the middle of a game. The kids would be devastated."

"Are you challenging me?" she asked.

"Yep. Loser buys the ice cream." Cole gave her a mischievous smile. "I should warn you that I played in high school."

As Jenna regarded the man in front of her, she wondered if maybe the pathway her DNA test had opened for her didn't involve her biological family after all. Maybe it was leading her to something else altogether.

Jenna grinned. "As the kids say, game on."

14

Eden

Eden sat on the back veranda and worked on her quilting project.

Earlier, she had tried the sewing machine in the inn, but controlling the speed of the machine and the material was anything but relaxing. So she opted for the old-fashioned method of hand stitching, even though it took longer and her stitches weren't exact. In the end, she would have something she'd made all by herself. Well, with a lot of coaching from The Busy Bees, but it was still something that was truly hers. And that was pretty exciting.

Despite Winnie's faith in her, Eden doubted she'd be done before the week was over, much less have time to start and finish a second quilt. She'd have to send Winnie and the other ladies a picture of the quilt when it was done, which gave her an idea that she should take pictures of her progress as she went along.

Eden reached into her pocket for her cell phone only to find . . . nothing.

Puzzled, she searched her project bag with no luck. Maybe it was in her purse in her room. Then she remembered that she'd left her phone in the car the day she'd arrived at the inn, and she hadn't once looked at it. How strange. Even stranger was the fact that Eden hadn't really missed the old ball and chain.

Eden went upstairs to retrieve her keys. She got them from her room, then went out to the car and grabbed her phone.

Back on the veranda, Eden took a deep breath. She'd been taking short walks around the inn and making it a point to get some form of exercise every day. But today had been the first time she had put any real effort into her movement, and she felt good. She could already feel the change from healthy food and having less stress in her life.

Eden spread out the quilt on the table and waited for the phone to power up. She reflected on how she'd been going stir-crazy until she walked into Spool & Thread. After spending a few hours with the quilting group, she'd found a calmness that she'd never known was possible. Gone was the need to live in the fast lane. Eden hadn't checked a news site in days and didn't know what was going on outside Magnolia Harbor. And she didn't even care.

A small laugh escaped her. Eden wasn't sure what had come over her or who she was anymore. What would happen next week when she returned to work? Would this new person remain in charge, or would the old Eden reemerge?

Before she could give it too much thought, her phone started beeping like mad.

Torn out of her reverie, she picked up the phone and gasped. Her in-box had exploded with messages, her text messaging had a hundred notifications, and she had more than twenty voice mails. What was going on?

After scrolling through the messages, she discovered that one of their biggest clients, a public figure, had been involved in a scandal, and her assistant, Fred, was in way over his head. Fred was threatening to quit. The client was threatening to sue. Her boss was begging her to help. Personally, she thought the client was kind of a spoiled jerk and deserved to get what was coming to him, but she couldn't let the company take the hit.

Eden packed up her quilting project and rushed to her room. For the rest of the day, she responded to e-mails, made phone calls, and crafted press releases. As she worked, she never noticed the time and ignored her rumbling stomach and the pounding at her temples.

She coached Fred through the press conference, feeding him the lines to settle the public. And she counseled the client on what he needed to do next—apologize, lie low, use common sense, and stay out of trouble.

Right before the client hung up, he told Eden, "I'm going to do what I was meant to do."

It was code for he'd do whatever he wanted and he didn't care about the consequences. They'd been down this road many times before.

As his words played over and over in Eden's head, her chest got tighter and tighter. Her breath got shallower and shallower.

The room started to spin.

The edges grayed.

She gripped the sides of the desk as tears rolled down her cheeks. Her mind screamed, *No more!*

Dimly, Eden became aware of someone knocking on her door, calling her name.

"Eden, it's Grace. Are you there?"

"Yes," she whispered.

The door opened slowly. "Eden!" Grace was at her side within seconds. "Are you okay? You're as white as a sheet. Let me check your pulse." She placed her fingers over Eden's wrist and searched her face. "Your pulse is racing. I think I should call 911. Can you tell me what else is going on? Is it your heart?"

"I was having trouble breathing, but it's better now," Eden said. It was true. The pressure around her chest had released. The air flowed through to her lungs and back out. This was different.

"I'm calling 911," Grace announced as she reached for her phone.

But Eden put a hand on Grace's arm to stop her. "No, I'm fine. I swear."

"You don't look fine. Just a minute." Grace hurried to the bathroom and returned with a glass of water and a hand mirror. "You're as pale as can be, and you're shaking."

Eden glanced in the mirror, winced, and set the offending object down. It was obvious that Grace had every reason to worry. "I'll be all right. Thank you. I think I need a bite to eat and maybe some fresh air."

"Let me talk to Charlotte." Grace called her sister and spoke quietly for a moment. When she hung up, she told Eden, "Charlotte is going to make you a plate and bring it up. How about dining with the doors open to the veranda?"

Eden nodded.

Grace opened the French doors to let in the cool November air and positioned the chair and end table where Eden could sit and enjoy the view but still be protected by the warmth of the house.

Before Eden could say or do anything, Charlotte arrived with a plate of food and a glass of water. Jenna and Winston came in behind Charlotte.

Winston made a beeline for Eden and sat down in front of her, wagging his tail as if waiting for an invitation to jump onto her lap.

"Don't bother her," Grace gently chided the dog. She bent to pick him up.

"He's not a bother," Eden said. "I welcome his company."

Winston whined until Grace set him on Eden's lap.

Eden laughed and cuddled him close. "You're such a sweetie."

"I hope you don't mind my stopping by," Jenna said to Eden. "I wanted to tell you that the appetizers you and Charlotte made were delicious. I was surprised you weren't at the social hour to enjoy them with us."

"I guess I lost track of time and forgot," Eden said, taking a sip of water. "But I'm glad you liked them."

"Are you kidding?" Jenna asked. "They were so good I had to buy Charlotte's cookbook so I'd have the recipes. I'm going to make them for my family at Thanksgiving."

Eden smiled. "That's nice to hear."

"Are we still on for dress shopping tomorrow?" Jenna asked.

"Oh yes," Eden said. "I can't wait."

"Great. I'll let you get some rest. See you in the morning." Jenna waved and left the room.

Eden took another sip of water and a bite of one of the appetizers they'd made that morning. They really were good.

"Jenna was really worried about you when you didn't join us downstairs," Charlotte told Eden. "We all were."

"I'm sorry," Eden said. "I didn't mean to worry everyone or put you both out, but thank you."

"I don't mean to be nosy, but what happened?" Grace asked, her soft voice conveying the concern of a friend.

Eden filled the sisters in on her day, including the scandal, the work, and the phone calls. "Honestly, everything was all right until the last call. When I hung up, I realized that nothing I said to that client was going to change him. I'm sure he'll behave for a week or two. If we're lucky, he'll stay out of trouble for a month. But then he'll go back to his old ways, and there will be another scandal for us to clean up."

Grace nodded.

"And then it hit me," Eden continued. "I'm him."

15

Jenna

It had taken every ounce of acting skill Jenna had not to show her concern over her new friend. It was the first time she'd seen Eden look anything less than perfect, and the woman's disheveled appearance and ghostly complexion were unnerving. Based on Grace and Charlotte's pinched expressions, she wasn't the only one who'd been alarmed.

Jenna had quickly determined that Eden didn't want to talk about whatever had kept her from joining them for hospitality hour. So Jenna had reconfirmed their plans for the next day and escaped to her own room.

Now Jenna grabbed the Magic 8-Ball off the fireplace mantel. She curled up in the chair and gazed out the window at Lake Haven. Her stomach was a mess of angry bees, which was ridiculous. Why should she be nervous about calling her sister? Isobel knew her every secret. They told each other everything.

She gave the ball a good shake. "Is Isobel mad at me?"

The little white die bounced around until finally one answer was clear: *Better not tell you now.*

Jenna let out a sharp laugh. "That's a yes if I ever heard one."

She picked up her phone and hit her sister's number. Putting off the call any longer would only make it harder. Besides, the DNA test results had been just as surprising to Isobel as Jenna. Until their parents had confessed the whole truth to them, her sister had refused to believe the proof in front of them. Even afterward, Isobel had adamantly stated it was impossible. Didn't the sisters share the same eyes and nose? And what about the weird little birthmark they both had on their upper arms?

Through it all, Isobel had stood by Jenna's side, sisters to the end.

Isobel deserved so much better than the treatment Jenna had dished out the last few weeks. Starting right now, she'd fix it.

If Isobel ever picked up the phone.

Finally, voice mail clicked on.

"Hey, Isobel, it's me. You're probably screening your calls to teach me a lesson. I don't blame you. I deserve it. Or maybe you're working. Please call me back. I don't care how late it is." Jenna paused to make sure her sister got the point. "I miss you. I miss my best friend and my sister. Love you."

Eden

Eden woke up early Thursday. Despite the chill in the air, she stepped out onto the veranda with a throw wrapped around her shoulders and watched the sunrise. Her whole body shivered as the sky turned a warm orange, promising another beautiful day in Magnolia Harbor. The shiver had less to do with the early morning temperature and more to do with the scare from the day before.

Over the past few days, Eden had made new friends and fallen in love with a little town that was starting to feel like home. She could see herself coming back in the spring to watch the trees unfurl their leaves and the flowers bloom. Then in summer to enjoy the sunlight soaking into her skin, to dive into Lake Haven and glide through the cool, clear water. And finally in the fall to witness nature's spectacular riot of colors.

Except yesterday was a reminder that she might not have many more seasons to enjoy unless she made some drastic changes immediately.

Before the sun had fully lit up the sky, Eden grabbed her phone and checked her messages. Her in-box was full again. With a deep sigh, she started on the first e-mail, giving Fred detailed instructions on how to handle each issue that was going on.

An hour later, her in-box was cleaned out, and her assistant had everything he needed from her to put out the fires their client had started with his poor judgment and impulse control. She also let Fred know that she would be unavailable the rest of the day.

Maybe she should shut down her phone again.

As Eden tossed the phone onto the bed en route to her private bathroom and the large tub that was calling her name, she mumbled, "I'm getting too old for this nonsense."

After taking a relaxing bath, Eden got ready and went downstairs for her next cooking lesson.

Winston greeted her at the kitchen door, dancing around her feet.

Eden laughed. "You're certainly in a good mood this morning."

"He just had his breakfast and a treat," Grace said with a grin.

"How are you feeling?" Charlotte asked. She poured a cup of decaf coffee and handed it to Eden.

"I'm still a little rattled from yesterday," Eden said, "but I'm feeling much better."

"I'm glad to hear it," Charlotte said.

"And I told my assistant that I'll be unavailable the rest of the day," Eden said, then took a sip of coffee.

"That's good," Grace said. "It sounds like you need a break from the stress at work."

Eden nodded. "So what are we making today?" she asked Charlotte.

"Baked apple oatmeal," Charlotte announced as she retrieved ingredients from the fridge.

"Sounds great," Eden said.

Winston yipped as if in agreement.

They all laughed.

As Eden helped prepare breakfast, she pushed away any thoughts of her job and checking her messages. Her phone was in her room, as it should be. She was on vacation, and she was sticking to her guns that she wouldn't do any more work for the rest of her stay.

When breakfast was ready, Eden, Grace, and Charlotte carried the food, plates, and utensils out to the veranda. Winston followed and sat at their feet.

A few minutes later, Jenna joined them. They spent some time on the veranda enjoying the fruits of their labor. Then Jenna and Winston left to work on his tricks for the dog show.

Eden and Jenna planned to meet up later after lunch to go dress shopping for the dance. Until then, Eden had some quiet time to work on her quilting project. Before coming to Magnolia Harbor and meeting The Busy Bees, Eden had always wondered why women toted their crafting projects everywhere. She didn't wonder anymore. She was hooked.

For the first hour, she worked steadily, lost in the project, enjoying the cool breeze and the warm sun.

As Eden snipped the thread and began another section, voices filtered through the house.

A moment later, Charlotte stepped out on the veranda followed by two women. "These ladies are here to see you," Charlotte told Eden. "They own—"

"The Serenity Boutique," Eden finished for her. "Good morning, Addie and Louise." Thankfully, their names came to Eden before Charlotte had to save her, although it did take a minute for her brain to kick in, which was unusual. "It's so nice to see you both."

"I'll bring out some iced tea and scones for you to munch on while you talk," Charlotte offered before disappearing inside the inn.

"This place is amazing," Addie said, glancing around.

"I'm almost expecting to see ladies in hoopskirts with parasols strolling across the lawn and gentlemen galloping up the drive on white horses," Louise added with a smile.

"I thought the same thing when I arrived," Eden said. "But they do have the cutest little dog who is very free with his snuggles. Maybe you'll get a chance to meet him if you stick around long enough."

Charlotte returned with a tray of scones, lemon curd, whipped butter they'd made that morning, molasses cookies, and a fresh pitcher of iced tea. "I need to step out, but if you ladies need anything else, Grace is at the front desk. Please enjoy."

"My, this place is more than amazing," Addie remarked. "Not only is the inn gorgeous, but the view is stunning and the staff is so friendly."

"That was Charlotte Wylde," Eden said. "She and her sister, Grace Porter, own the inn. Charlotte is a renowned chef and has a series of published cookbooks."

"Impressive," Louise said, taking a scone.

"They have her cookbooks for sale in the foyer," Eden said. "You should check them out before you leave." She had to give Charlotte a sales plug. After all, Charlotte had done so much for her.

Louise took one bite of her scone topped with lemon curd and groaned. "If this is any indication of the rest of her recipes, I'm definitely buying one of her books. Or all of them."

Addie sampled a cookie. "Me too." And then she laughed. "Contrary to what it seems like, we didn't come to interrupt your morning and eat all your snacks, although I'm not complaining."

Eden was curious as to what had brought the women to her, even as she enjoyed their company and found herself genuinely glad to see them.

Louise glanced at Addie and gave her a nod.

"After our talk with you at the coffee shop," Addie said, "we took another look at our website like you advised."

"I'm happy to hear it," Eden said.

"It was a mess," Addie continued. "We realized that you couldn't find the menu option easily on your phone. And things weren't organized as they should be."

"So we've redesigned the site," Addie said.

"Good," Eden replied. "Have you seen any uptick in traffic?"

Both ladies smiled and nodded.

"But that's not all," Louise said. "We started implementing some of the other ideas you gave us for our social media accounts. Nothing drastic, because we haven't had much time between the website redesign and getting ready for the festival, but traffic has already increased by 33 percent."

Eden smiled. "That's excellent."

"Are you kidding? It's incredible, and we owe it all to you. Thank you." Louise clasped her hands, tears shimmering in her eyes. "My husband said if this keeps up, I won't need to search for another job. Neither of us really wants that, as we'd like for me to be able to stay home with the kids."

"That's wonderful, and you're so very welcome," Eden said. "I'm glad I could help."

"You've already done so much, and you didn't even charge us," Addie said. "But we were wondering if we could share our ideas with you. Maybe you could tell us your thoughts or give us suggestions on how we can do better."

"We'll pay you," Louise added. "We don't have much, but we're hoping that will change soon."

Stunned, Eden sat at a loss for words, which was a rarity for someone in the public relations world. The suggestions she had given the ladies at the coffee shop were simple ideas that any first-year PR or marketing student would recommend. Never had she thought the women would seek her out for more advice or offer to pay her. She was flattered, of course, but she'd made a vow not to work for the rest of her stay. Especially after yesterday, she couldn't take a chance on breaking that oath.

However, this was different. When she'd been talking to Addie and Louise the first time, it hadn't even felt like work. True, they weren't paying her, so there hadn't been any pressure.

Eden didn't think it was the money that caused the stress in her job. No, the stress was caused by the long hours, the high demands from the clients, and her boss. The man never stopped and knew no boundaries, even when she was supposed to be on vacation. In addition, Eden was always pushing herself to work harder and take on more responsibilities than she should.

But talking to Addie and Louise was simply helping them out. Eden wouldn't even take their money, and then it wouldn't really be working. At least that was what she told herself.

With a chuckle, Eden gave in but made herself a promise that she'd take a nap before going shopping with Jenna.

Addie and Louise presented their ideas to Eden. For the next hour or so, the women refined, revised, and created new plans. Finally, the pair thanked Eden for her time and asked what they owed her.

Eden smiled and said, "I'll send you the bill later, but no worries. It'll be well within your budget."

She had no plans whatsoever to send them a real bill, but an idea was forming in her head. If she went through with it, Addie and Louise and the Serenity Boutique could play an integral role in Eden's future.

After the women left, Eden regarded her sewing project. It was coming along nicely. Maybe she'd even enter it in the arts and crafts contest on Saturday. Only a few more hours and she'd have it finished. A glance at her watch told her she could probably squeeze the time in before and after shopping.

She'd planned to take a nap, except she was anything but tired. Her mind was spinning in a dozen different directions while energy bounced along her nerves. Wasn't napping for babies, moms of babies, and sick people? She definitely didn't qualify for the first two, and she wasn't willing to be the third. Maybe she'd take a short walk and then try to rest.

This healthy lifestyle was going to kill her . . . of boredom.

Eden wanted to be out on the lake paddling a kayak. Or strolling down Main Street. Or dancing.

Sitting back, she tried to make sense of this renewed zest for life. That morning she'd been reeling from yesterday's scare. Now she was ready to take on the world. Last night she'd been drained from work. Today she'd done a different kind of work that had filled her soul with creativity, energy, light, and a love of life.

There wasn't any more time to analyze her revelation as Grace and Winnie stepped out onto the veranda with more iced tea and trays of food. It would be a miracle if her pants still fit by the end of the week.

"Grace and I were about to have lunch," Winnie said. "We knew you'd been out here working and thought you might be ready for something more substantial than cookies and scones."

"It's nothing fancy," Grace said. "Charlotte's off doing errands, but I do make a mean cup of vegetable soup, and I've been told my toasted cheese sandwiches are the best."

"Thank you," Eden said. "Everything looks delicious."

Grace and Winnie took their seats and passed around the steaming bowls of soup and plates of sandwiches with strawberries.

Eden took a bite of her sandwich, then grinned when she noticed that Grace's sandwich was cut into triangles.

Grace blushed when she saw that Eden was staring at her sandwich. "I'm not sure if I should blame the triangles on being a mom or because I like to dip my sandwich in my soup."

"Maybe you were simply letting your crafting side out," Eden suggested. "Either way, it's very tasty, and this china is beautiful."

"Thank you," Grace replied. "The china was my mom's. Every now and then I like to pull it out and use it for regular meals. It adds a nice touch."

"It definitely ups the atmosphere," Eden said. "Sitting here at this gorgeous inn, with the view and this lovely lunch, it's like being swept back in time. But I'm feeling underdressed, like I forgot my hat and gloves."

Grace and Winnie laughed.

"I'm glad I don't have to dress up every day." Grace filled all their glasses with iced tea. "After working in the corporate world for so many years and having to dress the part, opening the inn was like a breath of fresh air."

"Are you saying you don't miss high heels?" Eden teased.

"Goodness, no," Grace said. "At least now when I put them on it feels special. Maybe even a little magical."

"You both are too young to remember when a lady didn't leave her house in anything but a dress, heels, a hat, and gloves," Winnie said. "I certainly don't miss those days. Wearing hose and petticoats in South Carolina in the summer was awful. It's a miracle there weren't more of us passing out on the street from heat exhaustion."

"That's a good point," Grace said as she stirred her soup. "Of course, back then they thought women fainted because we were such delicate creatures."

"The truth is, we couldn't breathe with all those layers and corsets," Winnie said. "I like today's options better. If I feel like wearing a dress, I do. And if I feel like wearing jeans, I put those on and leave the house without a second thought."

"Hear, hear," Eden said.

All three women raised their glasses in salute.

"To progress," Winnie said.

"Speaking of progress, I can't believe how far you've gotten on your quilt," Grace told Eden. "You should enter it in the arts and craft contest. You could give Miss Lottie a run for her money."

"Who's that?" Eden asked.

"Lottie Duprie. She wins most of the craft contests in the county." Winnie rolled her eyes and sighed. "Bless her heart."

"I'm surprised one of The Busy Bees doesn't win," Eden said. "The quilts you make are stunning."

"Thank you." Winnie graced her with a warm smile. "I agree, but somehow Lottie usually beats us."

Grace laughed and covered her aunt's hands. "Winnie and the quilting group think it's because most of the judges are afraid of Lottie. She's a retired schoolteacher from the days when they used a yardstick to rule the class, and a lot of our judges had her for a teacher."

"People still have scars on their knuckles from that woman," Winnie added.

"Maybe I should pass on entering the arts and crafts contest," Eden said.

Grace and Winnie laughed.

"How about the baking contest instead?" Eden asked. "Charlotte taught me a muffin recipe today."

"That's probably a safer bet," Winnie said. "Lottie can't bake to save her life. She entered one time, but a judge broke his tooth on her biscuit and she never entered again."

Eden laughed. "I guess that settles it. I'll enter the baking competition."

"That sounds good," Grace said. "Feel free to use the kitchen tomorrow."

"Thank you. I might need a little assistance if you don't mind."

"We'll be more than happy to help," Winnie offered.

The conversation flowed as they ate their lunch and enjoyed each other's company.

Eden would miss all her new friends terribly after she returned to Atlanta. The thought stole the inner joy she'd experienced earlier, and that made another idea churn in her brain. What if she didn't return to Atlanta? What if she relocated? Maybe not to Magnolia Harbor proper but nearby. It was a thought worth giving more weight to, as she'd been happier in the last few days than she'd been in several years.

"Are you and Jenna going dress shopping for the dance?" Grace asked.

"We are." Eden checked her watch. She hadn't realized how late it was. "Actually, I expected her to meet me before now. Do you think she forgot?"

"I doubt that," Winnie answered. "Jenna told me Cole was taking her to the dance, and her eyes practically sparkled with excitement."

"She probably lost track of time," Grace said. "After she finished her session with Winston this morning, she was going to help out a neighbor with training a new puppy."

"She seems much happier than she was when she arrived," Eden commented. "Do you think that might have something to do with Cole? I know if I were many years younger and that man were paying attention to me, I'd be smiling."

"I'm pretty sure he has a lot to do with her dreamy smiles," Winnie said. "There's nothing like those first moments of a new romance."

Little nails clicking on the veranda signaled the arrival of Winston, who jumped into Winnie's lap and licked her cheek.

Winnie laughed. "Thank you, Winston. You sure know how to make a girl feel special. I love you too."

"He didn't want you to miss out on being romanced," Grace said with a smile.

"I still get plenty of that from your uncle," Winnie said. "We've been married a long time, but that man still surprises me with the most charming gestures. This morning he made me breakfast, and yesterday I came home from my walk to find flowers on the kitchen table."

"That's so sweet," Eden said.

The conversation turned to the festival and the dance. Eden wondered if Spencer had asked Grace to go with him, but she didn't want to pry into her hostess's personal life, so she didn't ask.

Thankfully, as a visitor, Eden didn't have to worry about having a date to the dance. Not that she'd be two-stepping even if she had a partner. But it would be nice to sway softly to the music with someone special once again.

Thinking about dancing brought back memories from long ago. One in particular forced Eden to remember the only man who had made her blush, stolen her heart, and then walked out on her.

But Eden didn't blame him. No one should have to be a third wheel in their own marriage. She'd been too gung ho making a name for herself at work. Anytime a volunteer was needed, Eden raised her hand. She put in long hours, worked on her days off, skipped vacations, and took it for granted that her husband would be there when she was ready.

Of course, he wasn't.

At the time of the divorce, Eden had attributed it to their youth. But as the years slipped by, she realized she needed to take ownership for her failed marriage.

Now at forty-two, she wondered if she still had a chance of finding love. Maybe someday, she'd be the one with the dreamy smile on her face.

Jenna

Jenna made her way through the crowd at the waterfront toward the game booths. Cole had commitments in Charleston, and since she had no other pressing engagements, she'd volunteered to man one of the booths.

As she walked, she thought of her shopping trip with Eden earlier in the day. Jenna had felt terrible that she'd lost track of time while training a puppy and had been late in meeting her friend.

But the excursion to Miss Millie's dress shop had been a success for both of them. Eden had bought a cranberry sweater dress, and it looked amazing on her.

Jenna couldn't believe that she'd found the perfect dress. Or rather Eden had found it for her. It had a crisscross-paneled bodice and a swingy skirt, and Jenna had felt pretty the moment she'd slipped it on. Eden told her that the deep green of the dress brought out the green in her hazel eyes and that Cole wouldn't be able to take his eyes off Jenna. Well, that remained to be seen.

She was excited about going to the dance with Cole on Friday and wearing her new dress. Too bad she had to wait another day.

Spotting Pastor Abrams and his Einstein hair was easy even with the mass of people filling the small grassy area surrounding the lake. Jenna waved and smiled at him, then continued toward the booths.

Grace and a few people Jenna didn't recognize were handling the games.

"How's business?" Jenna asked Grace, then motioned toward the balloon game without darts that she'd helped build.

"It's been a big hit with both parents and kids," Grace answered.

Jenna grinned. "That's great to hear."

Grace introduced Jenna to Zoe Caruthers and the other people assisting that night and explained that a game cost one ticket. Each child got three chances, and everyone received a prize. Glen was a soft touch and believed no one should go home empty-handed.

As if the thought conjured the man, the pastor joined the group. He greeted everyone warmly, then asked Grace, "Do you still need to leave?"

"I'm afraid so," Grace said. "Charlotte has a commitment away from the inn this evening."

He checked with the others before addressing Jenna. "I need to run and take care of some things. Would you mind working with Zoe for a little while?"

"Not at all," Jenna said. "For now, I think we can handle things between the two of us."

It was still early, and the park was already packed. But most people were strolling around or enjoying a snack or an early dinner from the food vendors. She'd also heard from Eden that there would be a band playing afterward. The stage was set up at the other end of the park, but she was sure they'd still get to enjoy the music and have a steady stream of visitors.

"Thank you," Glen said, and then he and Grace left.

Jenna took point on the basketball game, and Zoe stood next to her manning the no-dart balloon game. They really needed a better name than that. Maybe they could simply call it the balloon pop.

Before Jenna could get lost down the rabbit hole of renaming the game, two adorable boys ran up to the booth. One was of Hispanic descent and the other Asian.

The boys threw their arms around Zoe and yelled, "Mommy, can we play?"

Zoe laughed, kissed their faces, and let them squirm with anticipation. She introduced Jenna to her sons, Jordan and Cody, then asked the boys, "Where's your father?"

"He's still eating," Jordan said.

Zoe cupped Cody's chin and examined his face carefully. "Hmm, let me guess. Corn dogs and french fries with lots of ketchup?"

The kids nodded in unison.

"Do you have your tickets?" Zoe asked them.

Jordan and Cody, who could have been twins in their motions, pulled a string of red tickets from their front pockets.

"You two are going to be here for a while, aren't you?" Zoe teased. "Okay, but remember you have to let other kids play too, and no matter what, you're taking just one prize per game. We only have so much room at home."

The boys bent their heads together and whispered. Then they ran off to the cornhole game.

Zoe returned to the balloon pop game and her next customer, but the questions racing through Jenna's head must have shown on her face because Zoe asked, "Is everything okay?"

"Do you need to go with your kids?" Jenna asked. "If you do, I can watch both games."

"No, it's okay. Jordan and Cody won't take off. And while it seems like my husband, Matthew, isn't paying attention, he hasn't taken his eyes off those boys. He's like a hawk tracking his prey." Zoe pointed out her husband sitting at a picnic table with a clear view of the game booths.

The man was kicked back, eating fries, and his gaze didn't leave the boys except to scan the area around them for a second or two.

He also wasn't what Jenna had expected. His complexion was as light as Zoe's, matching neither boy.

"He seems very vigilant," Jenna remarked. "Is he a police officer?"

"Former military and current overprotective dad." Zoe handed a little girl her prize for popping all three balloons, then gave the next child his beanbags. "As you can tell, the boys aren't ours biologically, but that doesn't matter. They own us heart and soul. We'd give our lives for them."

There was a hint of an edge to Zoe's voice, as if she'd had to defend herself as a parent one time too many. It hadn't been Jenna's intent to hurt the woman or insult her. She was only making an observation.

Before Jenna could say anything else, a couple of older kids came up to her booth. Jenna passed out basketballs to them, then focused on Zoe again. "I understand."

Zoe gave her an apologetic glance. "I'm sorry. I didn't mean to sound short. People think because I didn't carry those boys that I'm not their 'real' mother. But you know what? Matthew and I walk the halls with them at two in the morning when they can't sleep or have fevers. We were there when they said their first words, and we caught them when they started to walk. We taught them to ride bikes and throw baseballs. We help them with their homework and deal with their schoolyard bullies. Those two guys are our lives. They're the reasons I get up in the morning and do what I do."

Listening to Zoe, Jenna realized that was how her own mom must have felt—like she'd checked off all the mom boxes, but someone would say she wasn't Jenna's real mom. Maybe that was one of the reasons why her parents never told Jenna the truth.

"I'm adopted too," Jenna blurted out. She couldn't believe that she'd told a complete stranger something so personal. It was completely unlike her, but somehow she didn't care. It felt good to admit the truth.

"So you get it?" Zoe asked. "The sideways glances? The questions? The silly and rude comments?"

Jenna needed to fess up the difference in their situations, but Zoe was on a roll and she didn't want to break the connection. "I'm sorry. I hope I didn't do that."

"No, you didn't," Zoe said. "I should apologize to you. I'm a little sensitive. A complete stranger approached me in the grocery store last week. She told me how lucky my boys were. She had it all wrong. Matthew and I are the lucky ones."

Jenna glanced over at Zoe's sons. They had already won a couple of prizes at the cornhole game, and now they dashed over to their dad. From the way the boys gestured at the food stands, it appeared they were trying to talk Matthew into getting dessert.

Zoe and Matthew exchanged glances that held a whole conversation, the way couples did, the way Jenna hoped someday she would with someone.

The three guys headed off toward the concessions, and the two women went back to the booths and their conversation.

"Those boys were a precious gift," Zoe went on. "They saved my life."

Zoe said these words with such conviction and matter-of-factness that Jenna stopped and faced the woman. "What do you mean?"

Zoe shook her head. "I don't know why I'm telling you all of this."

At first, Jenna had thought the pastor had put her and Zoe together because of their common denominator. But she was starting to wonder if forces higher up were at work.

She rested a hand on Zoe's arm. "I think it's because you know I need to hear your story. Not because I doubt that you're a great mom or a real mom. Maybe because I need to understand how I could have been considered a gift and not an embarrassment."

Zoe pulled her in for a quick hug, squeezing hard. "Even though I don't know your mom, I'm sure she would never consider you an embarrassment. Look at you. You're on vacation, and here you are volunteering your time to support our church. You know what kind of person does that? A good person. One who's kind and caring and puts others first. One who makes their parents proud."

Jenna laughed and wiped the tears from her eyes. "I know we're around the same age, but if my parents ever disown me, maybe you can adopt me."

"I do see some merit in that idea," Zoe replied. "I mean, you're past the diaper stage and the teenage rebellion phase. However, I have a feeling your parents are going to want to keep you. How about being an honorary younger sister?"

Jenna rolled her eyes. "I've already got one big sister telling me what to do, but I could always use another friend. You said the boys saved your life. Do you mind me asking how?"

Zoe took a deep breath and let it out slowly. "We got Jordan first. His parents had been killed in a car accident. They were friends of ours, and they had no other relatives. It was a simple decision. Cody came to us a couple of months later through the foster system. We immediately welcomed them both into our home. But there was so much red tape to get through."

"I understand that we need to protect the children," Jenna said. "But it's sad that it has to be so hard and expensive to get these kids into permanent homes."

"We were still going through the process of adopting Cody when my mom died. It was sudden, and I wasn't prepared. She was way too young. She'd just become a grandma. How could she be gone?"

Zoe and Jenna took tickets and gave out prizes as they talked. In the background, the band's music from the other end of the park played. Something upbeat that had the crowd singing along and didn't fit the discussion.

"I slipped into a deep depression after my mother passed," Zoe admitted.

"That's normal," Jenna said. "You can't beat yourself up over a natural reaction."

"But I had these two babies to take care of," Zoe protested. "Matthew stayed home for a while, but then he had to go back to work. I remember lying there in bed, listening to the boys as they cried. I could have sworn I heard my mom's voice telling me to get up and take care of her grandbabies."

Jenna didn't know what to say, so she kept quiet. She didn't believe in ghosts, but she did believe in the power of the mind and the body's will to survive.

"I walked into the boys' room and gazed at those sweet faces. Every time I wanted to go hide in my room or curl up and let the world pass me by, I'd see my boys and remember what a precious gift I'd been given. For so long I thought I'd never be a mother, but then I got Jordan and Cody. I decided I wasn't going to throw that away. I wasn't going to let them lose a second mom."

Tears slipped down Jenna's cheeks. Zoe was a little older than Jenna, which meant their moms were probably around the same age. The thought of losing her mom struck Jenna straight to the core. She couldn't breathe. She couldn't speak. All she could do was stand there and cry silent tears as pain shredded her heart.

"Are you all right?" Zoe asked.

Jenna nodded as she swallowed back the tears and heartache of Zoe's story. "I'm going to grab a drink. Do you want anything?"

Zoe declined and told her to take her time.

Instead of heading straight to the vendor booths, Jenna walked over to the water's edge and dropped down to watch the sun as it set. The sky was a clash of blues, pinks, and oranges. A couple of cranes swooped down and dived into the lake for their evening meal. Children giggled and played while their parents visited and shopped or simply enjoyed the evening.

It was the type of night meant for families.

Jenna suddenly wondered what she was doing here. *That's right. I'm avoiding my family, especially Aunt Lenore.*

Every family had to have one bad apple, and hers was her mother's aunt, who considered herself the family matriarch. Of course, so did the rest of the family, which meant the chance of the woman being uninvited was as slim as Jenna winning the lottery without buying a ticket.

But sitting on the cold ground and feeling sorry for herself wasn't going to solve her problems. Jenna needed to talk to her sister.

A second later, her phone rang.

Jenna smiled when she checked the screen. It was Isobel. "I'm so sorry," Jenna said as soon as she answered.

"Sorry I couldn't take your call last night," Isobel said. "I pulled a double, and there was an emergency. Are you okay?"

Turning to gaze at the lake, Jenna took a deep breath and told Isobel everything—where she was, why she'd left, how she felt about the whole thing with Aunt Lenore, and how she'd met Cole.

"Let me get this straight," Isobel said when Jenna was finished. "You're only about an hour away? I've been so worried."

"Yep. I'm sorry. I didn't mean for you or anyone else to worry."

"Mom and Dad have no clue, and let's leave it that way for now," Isobel said. "But maybe you could come home early."

It would mean missing out on her date with Cole, missing out on the dance, but Jenna was sure he'd understand. "I'll think about it."

18

Charlotte

Charlotte glanced around the pristine dining room at The Tidewater. Dean had gone upscale yet casual with white tablecloths, candles glowing in the center of each table, delicately scrolled silverware, and elegant glassware. It was the type of place where people could show up dressed to the nines or in smart casual attire and feel equally at ease. With the clear view of the lake, the restaurant was one of the most romantic spots to dine at in Magnolia Harbor.

Not that Charlotte had ever brought a date to The Tidewater. Given her and Dean's past, it would have been awkward at best. It had been less than a year since they'd gotten to the bottom of their misunderstandings from when they'd worked together at Le Crabe Fou in Charleston. And while she was pretty sure there had been a hint of a spark when they'd gone on a blind date months ago, he'd annoyed her too much at the time for it to be anything more.

But now, she wasn't so sure. Over the past few days, she'd seen another side of Dean. A softer side. A less arrogant side that was vulnerable, open, honest, and very human. It had her wondering if maybe that spark wasn't still glowing a tiny bit.

With a small groan, Charlotte pushed those thoughts away and turned back to the task at hand—getting through tonight's dinner rush with no mishaps.

One last examination of the dining room filled her with hope. She gave the signal, and the lights dimmed for the evening meal, creating the ideal atmosphere. It felt private, mysterious, and intimate.

Everything was ready to go.

Now to prep the staff and make sure they were all on the same page before she reinspected the kitchen.

Her phone buzzed in her pocket. It was Dean. Again.

He'd flown to St. Petersburg, Florida, early that morning against his mother's wishes. Dean and his brother, Marc, had decided it was time for a family reunion, so they could receive the results of their mom's post-op tests together as a family. Charlotte agreed with the plan. She knew that it was important for Dean and his brother to see their mother for themselves to make sure she was all right.

She read Dean's message. *Did Jack make it on time? He's perpetually late for his shift.*

At that moment, a man in his early twenties hustled through the dining room doors. He was slipping his tie over his head and adjusting it when he caught her eye and smiled. She'd bet that was Jack.

Everyone's here. How's your mom?

She's in great spirits. She smiled the whole time she scolded Marc and me for coming. I blamed Marc. That made her laugh, but she looks tired. She's resting now. I'm going to make her dinner.

Good. Give her my best and try to relax.

Call me if you have any questions or if any problems come up.

I will, but don't worry about it. I've run a kitchen before, remember? Now I need to go. I have work to do. Charlotte slid her phone back into her pocket.

The staff was already seated at a long table when she joined them. They'd been chatting softly among themselves but stopped when she sat down.

When Charlotte had managed the kitchen at Le Crabe Fou, she would bring the staff in early for dinner. It was a good chance to connect, and it also gave everyone the opportunity to taste the daily specials. It was hard for the waitstaff to recommend food they hadn't tried. She was surprised to find out that Dean had continued the tradition at The Tidewater.

"Hi, everyone." Charlotte cleared her throat, suddenly needing a glass of water. "Dean had to leave town for a couple of days. I'll be filling in for him."

"Why didn't he have Ruby fill in?" asked a young woman in a waitress uniform.

"He didn't say," Charlotte answered, then smiled at the entire staff. "For those of you who don't know me, I'm Charlotte Wylde, co-owner of the Magnolia Harbor Inn. Before that, I was the head chef at Le Crabe Fou, where Dean and I worked together."

"You didn't just work together there," Annie, the commis chef, pointed out. "You were the head chef, and Dean was the sous-chef. She was his boss." The young woman stared down at the table after she said it, as if that explained everything.

"So—" Before Charlotte could say anything else, her phone buzzed again. Dean.

Please remind the hostess that the Greenes will be in tonight to celebrate their thirtieth anniversary. Sit them at table 8 so they have a lake view and the fireplace. Mr. Greene's arthritis has been bad lately. Also, their wine is on the house.

Charlotte passed Dean's message on, and she noticed that the hostess made a note in her phone.

"Okay, as I was saying, tonight's specials are autumn beef stew, roast chicken with wild mushroom sauce served over—"

Once again, the phone buzzed, cutting her off.

Charlotte sighed. "Just a minute."

Also, a heads-up. Peter, a busboy, has a crush on Beth, a waitress. Keep an eye on him, as he tends to follow her around like a lost puppy and gets behind in his work.

Charlotte scanned the name tags of the staff members until she found Peter. Sure enough, the young man was sitting across from Beth with a dopey grin and love written all over his face. The poor guy was going to get his heart broken, as Beth paid no attention to him and was fully focused on Jack. She inhaled deeply and counted to ten. Restaurants were a hotbed of drama. How could she have forgotten that?

"Dean wishes you all a great night, and he knows you'll make him proud." Before the phone could interrupt once more, Charlotte ran through the rest of the specials and her expectations. "Enjoy your meal. I'll be in the kitchen if you need me."

Slipping into the kitchen, Charlotte let the familiar scents soothe her ravaged nerves. The rich aromas of beef, red wine, garlic, and bacon from the stew had her stomach grumbling in protest, as she hadn't eaten in hours. She dipped the ladle into the stockpot and filled a cup. The savory depth of the broth brought her taste buds to life. The meat melted on her tongue, and the vegetables were fork-tender. In other words, it was perfect.

It had been years since Charlotte had worked in a restaurant, but this was one of her favorite moments. The calm before the storm when the kitchen was quiet and all hers, when she could envision the night to come and the anticipation of the diners' reactions to her food. Of course, it was slightly different tonight. This wasn't her kitchen, and it wasn't her name on the menu. The diners were not expecting Charlotte. She'd have to make sure each and every one of them left satisfied.

Thankfully, Dean's staff ran like a well-oiled machine. Ruby took no prisoners. The sous-chef had eyes in the back of her head and a skill to anticipate problems that bordered on magical.

The dining room stayed steady and full, and they made it halfway through the night without any mishaps.

During a lull, Charlotte and Ruby took a few minutes to discuss the menu for the next couple of days.

"I'm not sure when Dean will be back," Charlotte said. "We talked about the menu, but we didn't finalize it before his flight."

"That's because he doesn't plan the menu ahead of schedule," Ruby said. "He decides that morning, usually while he's at the farmers market. I understand that's what you used to do at Le Crabe Fou."

"How did you know that?" Charlotte asked.

"Dean told me. He said you'd always wait until you saw what was in stock that morning so everything would be at its freshest."

"I still do that sometimes when I'm planning for our guests at the inn." It didn't surprise Charlotte that Dean did the same thing. They saw each other often at the morning market. But it did surprise her that he shared details of their time together at Le Crabe Fou with his staff.

"If you decide tonight what you want for tomorrow's specials, I can do the morning shopping for you," Ruby said. "That way you can take care of your guests at the inn."

If what Charlotte had seen that evening was any indication of Ruby's normal work, the woman was ready for a promotion. Charlotte would love to let her come up with the next day's specials and do the shopping, but that would violate the trust Dean had placed in her. However, there might be something else she could do that would benefit them all.

"Thanks for the offer," Charlotte said. "Let's talk more after the shift. I'd like to hear your ideas."

Ruby appeared startled. She dropped her gaze and shuffled her feet. Finally, she met Charlotte's eyes. "Only Dean decides on the specials."

"Yes, but I'd like your input," Charlotte said. "You work here and know the menu, and you're aware of the specials Dean has had recently. He's not here to fill me in, and I don't want to bother him while he's away."

Ruby nodded. "He's a good chef to work under. Thank you."

"Why are you thanking me?" She hoped it wasn't for asking Ruby for her opinion. Surely Dean didn't ignore his second-in-command.

"Because Dean said you taught him how to be a good boss, a better chef, and a better person."

Words escaped her. What could Charlotte say to a claim like that? Yes, as head chef it had been her responsibility to teach her team to do their jobs better, to work together better, but never had Dean let on that he was actually listening to her.

The man had a healthy ego. When they'd worked together, he tended to second-guess her orders, because he always knew a better way and had no problem sharing with the group. But if she believed what she was hearing, he had been listening. So why was he still pushing her buttons?

Annie brought over a fresh batch of peeled and chopped apples for the chicken entrée. "He talks about you all the time. When I'm doing something wrong, he'll say, 'If Charlotte was here, she'd smile and patiently show you how to do it all over again. I don't have that kind of patience, so watch closely.'"

"No way." Charlotte glanced from one woman to the other, embarrassed. "He doesn't do that."

Both women snorted and nodded.

Being in the spotlight wasn't what bothered Charlotte. It wasn't exactly new to her. She'd been well-known in the restaurant business during her time as head chef at Le Crabe Fou. And now her stream of cookbooks kept her in a tiny spotlight in the culinary world.

What bothered her was the way the staff said Dean talked about her. It sounded like they read more into Charlotte and Dean's relationship than what was there. They were just friends. And Magnolia Harbor was a small town. Neither she nor Dean needed another round of rumors powering the gossip mill. With her luck, she'd get another of Dean's crazy stalkers trying to ruin her again.

Thankfully, when that had happened the two of them had gotten to the bottom of the mystery and resolved the issue before her publisher had dropped her cookbook contract. She didn't imagine Chow Bella Publishing would look kindly on a second round of bad publicity.

"Hey, Charlotte." Jack poked his head into the kitchen. "If you have a moment, the Greenes would like a word with you."

"I'll be right there." Charlotte walked over to the computer to pull up the couple's order for the night. Both had selected the roast chicken with wild mushroom sauce over risotto and the spiced pear-cranberry cobbler for dessert.

Charlotte took a minute to clean up. She washed her hands, ran a washcloth over her face, and slipped on a clean chef's jacket. Then she let Ruby know she was stepping out into the dining room. Traffic had slowed. Once she had talked with the Greenes, it would probably be a good idea to check with a few other diners to make sure everyone was happy.

Jack pointed to the table before disappearing. Was he busy or making a quick getaway? Charlotte wasn't sure which. He'd given her no clue as to the couple's mood or the origin of their request. She knew the Greenes from church. Most of the time they were pleasant enough, but Joseph could be a bit cantankerous, and his wife, Betsy, had a reputation of being overtly critical of the options available during the Christmas cookie exchange.

Charlotte approached their table and smiled. "It's so lovely to see you both. I understand congratulations are in order."

"Thank you," Betsy said. "But what on earth are you doing

here? Have things gotten so slow at the inn that you've had to take a second job?"

"No, not at all," Charlotte answered. "I'm simply helping Dean tonight."

"Where is he?" Joseph glanced past her toward the kitchen doors. "I asked to speak to the chef, not his assistant."

Charlotte smiled. She'd been down this road before. There were still some people like Joseph who thought all chefs had to be men. "Dean is out of town for a family situation. I'm sure you understand given how important family is to the two of you. Thirty years is impressive. I hope someday I'm as lucky as the two of you are."

"Oh, thank you," Betsy replied. "That's a sweet thing to say. How are your sister and your aunt and uncle doing? I missed choir practice this week."

Charlotte took a few minutes to catch Betsy up on the local comings and goings as well as church news. She reminded the couple that they still needed volunteers to man the booths for the festival before returning to the business of dinner. "Did you enjoy your risotto tonight?" she asked.

Betsy glanced at her husband. "We did. It was some of the best risotto we've ever had." There was something in her voice that caught Charlotte's attention. The woman was holding back, almost like she was afraid to tell her the truth and hurt Charlotte's feelings.

"Was the chicken okay?" Charlotte asked. "Not too dry?"

"No, it was delicious. As was the cobbler." Betsy smiled. "I hope you're willing to share the recipe. It would make a nice addition for Thanksgiving dessert."

"Of course. I'd be happy to," Charlotte said. "I'm glad you enjoyed your meal, but was there a reason you asked to see the chef? If something was wrong with the food, you can tell me."

Joseph mumbled something under his breath that sounded like no and waved her off.

Charlotte held her ground. If there was a problem, she'd fix it.

"It's just we weren't expecting you," Betsy explained. "No one said anything about you working here now."

"It's only temporary." Charlotte could hear the wheels on the rumor mill starting up, and she guessed it would be in full motion before she even got home. Perhaps she should send Grace a warning text.

"We have a tradition," Betsy continued. "We come here on each of our birthdays and our anniversary. And at the end of each meal we ask for the chef and let him know how the meal was. When you showed up instead of Dean, it kind of threw us off." She laughed softly.

"Dean was very sorry he missed you tonight given the special occasion," Charlotte told them. "I'll be sure to let him know that you asked for him."

"Please thank him for the wine," Betsy said. "It was wonderful."

"I certainly will," Charlotte said.

"And please send him our best," Betsy added. "You are a divine chef, and we truly enjoyed our meal."

"Thank you. And happy anniversary." Charlotte excused herself and stopped by a few more tables in the dining room to speak with the patrons. Everyone seemed pleased with their food.

The rest of the night flew by without incident. Then Charlotte and Ruby sat down and brainstormed a few ideas for nightly specials dependent on what Ruby found at the market in the morning. The sous-chef seemed nervous and thrilled to be given this chance to step up her game. Since all the dishes were recipes Charlotte had created, she didn't feel like she'd broken Dean's trust.

Charlotte left Ruby to finish closing up. When Charlotte reached her car, her phone rang. Who would call at midnight? Concerned something had happened at the inn, she scrambled in her bag for her phone and checked the screen. It was Dean. She answered.

"Hi, Charlotte." Dean's warm voice soothed her jangled nerves.

"Is everything okay?" she asked. "Your mom?"

"Sleeping soundly. Me, not so much."

"Your sleep cycle isn't set to shut down for the night yet. It's still early for you," Charlotte reminded him. She unlocked the car and slipped inside, where she could get out of the chilly breeze and turn on the heat.

"How did things go tonight? Any problems?" he asked. Concern and guilt laced his voice.

"Everything ran like clockwork," Charlotte assured him. "You've got a great team."

"Did the Greenes like the wine?"

"Yes, they wanted me to thank you. And they send you their best. Your absence was definitely noticed by everyone. So, did you call to make sure I hadn't burned your place down?"

"Something like that," Dean said with a chuckle. "Thanks again for doing this for me."

She laughed. "Thanks for trusting me with your kitchen."

"I knew it was in good hands."

Eden

Last week, life in the slow lane would have made Eden climb the walls out of boredom. She chuckled as she worked on her quilt on the veranda outside her suite. She was actually taking the time to revel in the glorious morning and the view of Lake Haven. Oh, how her life had changed.

It had been days since she'd set her alarm clock. She'd even managed to sleep until eight that morning. It might not sound late to most people, but it was a big deal to Eden, who used to wake up at four. She shook her head at the thought. It was like she was living in the lap of luxury these days. It had been twenty-four hours since she'd checked her e-mail. Not an easy feat. She'd spent the past twenty years at her clients' beck and call. This whole unplugging thing wasn't as easy as it sounded, but Eden liked it.

Instead of putting out PR fires or drafting apology letters and press releases, Eden had spent yesterday shopping and laughing with Jenna and helping the ladies of the Serenity Boutique. She'd been forming real connections. And she'd never felt more alive.

There hadn't been a single moment when her heart raced too fast or she couldn't catch her breath. No shaking limbs or loss of strength. No blurred vision or weird spots dancing before her eyes.

It was like turning back the clock and getting a do-over.

Eden had also started to wonder what else was out there for her. Wasn't twenty years of fixing other people's mistakes long enough? Especially when they were on a rinse-and-repeat cycle and made the same mistakes only on a larger scale.

She had skills and talent, but did she have the courage to let go of the familiar and break out on her own?

Her phone rang, interrupting her thoughts. It was Fred. For her assistant to call, he must be getting desperate.

Eden reluctantly picked up the phone. "You do know the purpose of a medical leave of absence, correct?"

"I'm sorry," Fred said. "I wouldn't have called if it wasn't an emergency. But we have a problem that only you can handle."

Eden sighed. "Okay, what's going on?"

Clearly panicked, Fred explained the whole sordid mess to her. A well-known celebrity Eden had personally signed many years ago had been caught in a major scandal. An arrest warrant was being issued for the man, and there was talk of federal prosecution and time in prison. Of course, their client claimed to be innocent, said to have thought the deal he'd made was on the up-and-up. He was a nice man, not the sharpest crayon in the box, so he probably was telling the truth.

Still, it wasn't her problem, nor was there anything she could do to change what had happened. It was a little hard to put a positive spin on an arrest warrant, other than to show how easy it was to get duped. But Fred was more than capable of taking care of the situation.

"Listen to me," Eden said. "First, you need to breathe. Take a deep breath in, and let it out."

When her assistant murmured on the other end of the line, she knew his moment of panic had receded.

"Second, you've got this under control," Eden said firmly. "It's a problem that you'll need to handle, and I have complete faith in you."

"Okay, but I need your guidance," Fred said, then ran through some ideas. It sounded more like he was simply thinking out loud than asking for her approval.

After he was done, Eden said, "See? You've got this. If I've ever made you feel like you couldn't do this job or you needed my assistance, I'm sorry. You're ready to move up to executive communications manager. In fact, I'm going to recommend that you get promoted."

When the call ended, Eden felt like an enormous weight had been lifted from her shoulders and conscience. She realized she'd found her replacement. It seemed like that was step one, but she didn't know if she was ready for step two.

Tired of driving herself crazy with her own thoughts and company, Eden considered her options. Maybe she'd drive into town and enjoy the Holidaze Festival. Or stop in at Spool & Thread to find her next project pattern and supplies. She could always drive to Charleston and check out the real estate market.

After dropping off her quilt in her room, Eden went downstairs and stepped out onto the front veranda. Still considering what to do to occupy her time, she sat down on the front steps.

Almost as if he could sense her need, Winston appeared and climbed into her lap.

"Have you come to save me from myself today?" Eden asked. "My knight in shining armor?"

The dog wagged his tail as if to say yes.

She laughed. "We'll have to call you Sir Winston from now on."

"Oh no, please don't." Grace walked along the front of the house pushing a wheelbarrow. She grinned. "If you give him a title, he'll expect the treatment to go along with it."

Eden cuddled the dog. "I have a feeling he's already treated like the king of the mansion."

"That he is." Grace sat down, pulling off her gloves. "I'm surprised you're here. I thought you would have gone over to enjoy the festival. There's a really good band playing today. Judith's husband, Ken, is in it. Did you meet Judith at Spool & Thread the other night?"

Eden nodded. Judith was a lovely woman originally from Georgia who had made Eden feel right at home the minute she'd walked into the store. "She mentioned it to me. I might go over later. I was working on my quilt, but then I started feeling restless. I'm not sure if I need people or something to do or both."

"The festival will fill that need," Grace said. "Or, if you don't mind getting your hands and knees dirty, you're welcome to help me with the flower beds. It's nothing exciting. I'm only deadheading flowers and spreading fresh mulch." She smiled. "Although I'm sure Sir Winston would be thrilled if you spent the rest of the day snuggling with him. Jenna wore him out this morning with his training session."

As much as Eden loved the dog, she gave him one last cuddle and stood up. She needed to burn some energy. "I'd love to join you."

"Great. Follow me." Grace pushed the wheelbarrow to the side of the house, then handed Eden a pair of gloves from a basket that was already there. "Feel free to do as much or as little as you want. If you start getting tired, I want you to stop, okay?"

"Yes ma'am," Eden said with a smile, slipping on the gloves. "How's Winston's training coming along? Do you think he'll win the blue ribbon in the dog show Saturday?"

Grace popped off a handful of dead flowers before tossing them into the wheelbarrow. "He might. Our knight is a smart boy, and Jenna seems really pleased with his progress. I feel guilty that she's been working on her vacation, though."

"Don't worry," Eden said. "She's been enjoying herself. We both have. It's like we've found our home away from home. Besides, I think being with dogs is her happy place." She winked. "Well, that and being with Cole."

Grace dusted off her hands and laughed. "I did notice how she lights up like a Christmas tree around him. To be honest, I never get tired of watching people fall in love. There's so much promise. So much hope and potential."

"It does seem like anything is possible during the first few weeks of a new relationship," Eden said wistfully.

Grace studied her. "Are you all right?"

"I'm fine," Eden answered. "I was just reminded of the early days of my marriage."

Grace placed a hand on her heart, her expression stricken. "I'm sorry. That was insensitive of me."

"No apologies needed. My marriage ended a long time ago. Besides, I've still got hope that someone is out there for me." Eden paused. "Actually, I've been thinking there might be a lot of new things out there for me."

Grace dropped the bag of mulch between them and raised her brows. "That sounds intriguing."

"My meeting with Addie and Louise, the ladies from the Serenity Boutique, really got me thinking. What if I used my PR skills for something good? Not that I'm out defending evil now, but what if I focused on small businesses instead?"

"What do you have in mind?" Grace asked.

"I could act as a consultant," Eden said. "I could give them advice on how they can up their game, bring their business into the limelight, and make it shine. Show them how to get their name out into their community so that when people need their services or products, that's where they go first instead of big chain stores."

"I like where you're going with this idea." Grace dumped the bag of mulch, and the two of them started spreading it out. "Do you have any marketing in your background?"

"It was my minor," Eden answered. "Plus, with my job, I've had to keep an eye on the current trends. I think for now my focus would be on getting the client seen. I love public relations."

"I'm not trying to be nosy, but did the doctor tell you to quit or find another line of work?" Grace asked.

Eden shook her head. "After I gave him so much flak over taking this week off, he probably knew if he had, I would have simply ignored him."

"I'm not so sure about that given our current conversation. I think you only needed time to figure it out in your head and your heart." Grace took off her gloves and pushed a stray hair behind her ear. "You're not the same person who arrived here on Saturday."

"I'm not?" Eden sat back on her heels. She'd thought the same thing, but she didn't realize it was outwardly noticeable.

Grace looked Eden up and down. "When you arrived, you were a mass of energy. I kind of worried that you'd burst through the walls. This morning you seemed like you could have sat on the veranda and happily sewn all day."

"I was doing that until work called," Eden admitted. "Each time I've had to deal with my job this week, it's left me feeling agitated and unhappy. Talking to Addie and Louise was the exact opposite."

"Are you locked into a contract with your company?" Grace asked.

"No."

"What's holding you back from leaving your job?"

Eden had been giving that question a lot of thought all morning, and one word kept popping up over and over again. Even now, Eden didn't know if she could admit it, if she should voice that emotion. What if by doing so she was giving it power?

Grace dropped her gloves into the basket. "Come on. Let's go see what Charlotte left us to snack on in the kitchen while you think about it. I find that sometimes if I don't force the answer, it's easier to find it."

The two women walked around to the front of the house to find Winston napping on the front steps. He cracked an eye open and watched them head to the door.

Grace stopped and glanced back at the dog. "You aren't telling me you're too tired for a snack, are you?"

The dog jumped up and ran through the doorway, barking and dancing in circles.

Eden wasn't sure what Winston's snack consisted of, but if Charlotte made it, she knew it would be delicious.

Both women laughed and followed the dog to the kitchen, where they found a basket of pumpkin mini muffins and an assortment of herbal teas. Eden picked vanilla tea, and Grace selected cinnamon-apple. Winston even had his own banana-pumpkin muffins.

Once the snacks were doled out, Grace suggested they enjoy their treats in the living room. She flipped on the gas fireplace, even though it was sixty degrees outside. The fire set the mood. They were a couple of friends sharing secrets, discussing important life decisions in a safe space.

They sat on opposite couches, choosing the ends closest to the fireplace.

Winston finished his snack, then hopped onto his dog bed in front of the fire, turned around three times, and curled up with a deep sigh.

I hear you, little buddy, Eden thought.

"I have an answer to your question." Eden concentrated on tearing her mini muffin into bite-size pieces. "What's holding me back is fear of failure. What if I quit my job, start my own business, and fail miserably?"

"A very wise woman once said, 'You must do the thing you think you cannot do.'"

"Eleanor Roosevelt." Eden popped a morsel into her mouth. "Your sister is a genius in the kitchen. And I'm sure if Mrs. Roosevelt were here, she'd tell me to follow my fear."

Grace set her empty plate on the coffee table. "As wise as Mrs. Roosevelt was, her advice might not be right for you. Only you can decide that. You need to find your own path. Granted, the first one you head down might not lead to the destination you have in mind. You might even have to backtrack and go down a different path. But if you keep trying, you'll eventually find the right path that will lead you to happiness and better health."

Eden nodded as she considered Grace's advice. Then she asked, "Do you ever miss your high-powered job?"

Without missing a beat, Grace responded, "Not at all."

A thought drifted into Eden's mind. *Could I ever feel the same way?*

20

Jenna

Jenna had spent the morning in her room debating if she should stay or go.

She'd flipped the Magic 8-Ball over again and again, and no matter which question she asked, it gave her the same answer.

Yes—definitely.

How could she stay and go at the same time?

Her heart was torn. Part of her wanted to go home, see her family, hug her parents, and tell them everything was all right. The other part wanted to stay and spend the last couple of days of her vacation in Magnolia Harbor and enjoy every minute she could with Cole, who was visiting for the weekend. The truth of it was she was being a bit selfish by putting off dealing with her family drama. But she also had a feeling that she was meant to end up in this place.

Maybe Jenna was caught in one of those weird, quirky schemes of life where all the pieces were leading her to Magnolia Harbor so she could meet her one true love. Jenna laughed at her silliness. The lack of sleep was definitely getting to her. She didn't believe in predestiny or fate or magic. If any of that really did exist, the silly black ball would give her a clear answer.

As she tossed the Magic 8-Ball up and down, she had to admit that it all hadn't been a lost cause. The ball had told her to go out with Cole, and that decision had been a good one. Winnie was clearly on to something there.

Jenna stuck the ball into a corner of her suitcase because her next move would have to be one that she'd decide on her own.

Or not, because at that moment the phone rang. It was her sister.

"Bad news," Isobel said. "I've got to work tomorrow morning, so I need you to come home and help Mom with the cooking. She can't do it all by herself."

Her sister didn't know when to stop. Jenna had already told Isobel she'd think about coming home earlier, but that didn't seem to be good enough. "You're stooping to a guilt trip?" She had been leaning toward going home until her sister pulled that stunt.

"I'm not lying, if that's what you're implying," Isobel said. "We're short-staffed. Even nurses get the flu."

It was then that Jenna heard the truth in Isobel's words, heard the exhaustion in her voice. She realized what she had to do. "Sorry. I didn't sleep well last night. You know me. Anything less than a solid eight hours and I'm cranky. Are you feeling okay?"

"Yeah, I'm okay."

"I'll be at Mom and Dad's tomorrow morning," Jenna said. "And I'll see you when you get off work. I'll even save you an extra piece of cherry pie."

"Thanks. I knew I could count on you," Isobel said, then disconnected.

Jenna's mom would be up at five to start baking and cooking for the day. The woman didn't believe in prebaking. Everything had to be fresh for her family. Since it was an hour and a half drive from Magnolia Harbor to her parents' house and only a twenty-minute drive from her place, checking out early would be the logical thing to do. But she'd miss going to the dance with Cole tonight.

After throwing all her clothes into her suitcase, Jenna headed downstairs to find Grace or Charlotte to tell them the news. She felt bad about leaving two nights early.

Winston met her halfway down the curved staircase for his usual ear scratch. She was going to miss her new friend.

Grace was alone at the front desk. Upon seeing the suitcase, she did a double take and set down her pen. "Is everything all right?"

"Yes, everything is fine." For the first time in weeks, Jenna could answer truthfully, and it was like having the weight of the world lifted from her chest. "I can't begin to thank you and Charlotte enough for a wonderful stay. It was exactly what I needed, and it felt more like spending time with friends. I'm going to miss everyone so much, especially this sweet guy." She scooped Winston up and cuddled him in her arms.

Grace frowned as she glanced at her computer. "I thought you were staying until Sunday. Did I have your reservation mismarked?"

"No, that was my original plan, but some family stuff has come up," Jenna replied. "My sister is a nurse and she got called into work, so I need to cut my time short. I'm so sorry for any inconvenience."

"Don't worry about that. I just hope everyone is okay." Grace's gentle voice was filled with genuine concern.

"Yes, everyone's fine. It's kind of a long, complicated story," Jenna said. "But I'll come back sometime and give you all the nitty-gritty details. Bottom line, thanks to my stay here and all the wonderful people I've met, everything's great."

"Will you get a chance to stop by the festival before you leave?" Grace asked. "I think Charlotte is going to be there in a bit. I know she'd love to say goodbye."

"I have a few hours left until I need to go. I'd like to thank Pastor Abrams too, and I'd like to say goodbye to a certain someone." Jenna felt heat creep into her face at the thought.

Grace smiled, obviously knowing exactly who she was talking about. "Well, let's get you checked out. And I'm looking forward to hearing your story next time you visit."

Jenna packed up her car and gave Winston another scratch behind the ears, along with a pep talk for the dog show. "If you have a few minutes, I'll give you a quick rundown of Winston's tricks."

"Of course," Grace said.

Jenna retrieved the dog treats and showed Grace how Winston had learned to wave hello, spin in a circle, and then take a bow, along with a few other feats. He performed every trick perfectly.

"That was wonderful," Grace said to the dog. "And you don't even need much direction."

"Just a little encouragement," Jenna said as she gave Winston a treat.

Grace laughed. "Thank you for spending so much time with Winston and teaching him these great tricks."

"It was my pleasure," Jenna said. "Good luck at the show. Please let me know how it goes."

"I will," Grace promised. She picked up the dog and rubbed his ears.

Jenna waved to Grace and Winston, then headed into town.

By the time Jenna found parking and arrived at the waterfront, the festival was in full swing, which given it was still midday on Friday surprised her. As she searched for Glen, she noted that many of the attendees had silver hair. She had seen quite a few shuttle buses. The church must have arranged for the nearby senior homes to bring their residents out for an early-bird special.

She made her way around clumps of people and smiled at a few she recognized from her time spent volunteering. Unfortunately, in this crowd the good pastor didn't stand out nearly as much as he normally did—everyone was snowy, and most of the men seemed to sport the Einstein hairstyle. As she was about to give up and leave, she heard her name.

Cole.

She spun around and smiled to find her two favorite men in Magnolia Harbor. "Just the guys I hoped to find."

"It must be our lucky day," Glen said.

"Actually, can I talk to you for a moment . . . alone?" she asked the pastor.

Cole touched her elbow gently, but his smile was filled with understanding. "I'll grab us a table for lunch. Is that okay?"

"That sounds great," Jenna said. "I'm starving."

"How about I pick up lunch too?" Cole suggested. "Any requests?"

"Surprise me."

Cole grinned. "Okay, but don't forget that you asked for a surprise."

After Cole left, Jenna asked the pastor, "He's not going to make me eat some kind of deep-fried bug, is he?"

He laughed. "More like a pimento cheeseburger."

"I can handle that," she replied. "But I'm not sure about some exotic delicacy that's been deep-fried."

"I'm with you," Glen said. "So how are things going?"

"I'm afraid I need to head back to Charleston today," Jenna said. "I'm sorry that I won't be able to help out the rest of the weekend. But I wanted to say thank you."

"You've done so much this week," the pastor said. "It's me who should be thanking you."

"No, you kept me busy, and that allowed me to clear my head so I could find my way to the correct path." Jenna stole a peek at Cole, allowing a small smile to give away more than she intended. "Or maybe I should say correct paths."

"You are always welcome in my house." Glen chuckled. "But I'd better let you go because Cole is heading toward the deep-fry tent."

Jenna bid the pastor goodbye and went to head off Cole before she ended up trying something strange.

By the time she reached him, he was already holding a tray. "What did you order?" she asked.

Cole moved the tray so she couldn't see what was on it. He had a huge grin on his face.

Her insides quivered with trepidation. *Oh, please don't be worms. Or crickets.*

Finally, he showed her the tray. "Gyros, parmesan fries, and sweet tea."

"Nothing deep-fried?" Jenna asked, eyeing the food.

"No, but now I'm wondering what to get for dessert," Cole said, motioning to the menu on a large chalkboard. "The chocolate-covered frog legs sound good."

"Please tell me you're kidding." She closed her eyes and tried not to picture any frogs.

"They also have chocolate-covered bacon, but I was thinking the deep-fried cookie or cheesecake would be a better choice." Cole chuckled as he led them to a nearby table.

Jenna laughed with him. "Who puts chocolate on bacon? I mean, yeah, I see bacon and eggs. Or bacon and cheese. Bacon on salads or potatoes. And chocolate with nuts or peanut butter because you can't beat chocolate with peanut butter. But chocolate and bacon is plain wrong."

"See, I knew there was a reason why I liked you." He took a bite out of his gyro and gestured toward her untouched lunch. "Was it something I said? If you don't like the gyro, I can get you something else."

"No, I have some bad news." She filled him in on her call with her sister and her decision to go home early. "I'm sorry about missing the dance this evening and messing up your plans. I know you took off early to spend the weekend with me."

"It's no big deal. I understand," Cole said. "Do you have to leave right now, or can you stay for a little while?"

Technically the time was hers and she could stay longer, but Jenna didn't want to get home too late. Four o'clock in the morning came awfully early.

"I'll stick around on one condition." She flashed him what she hoped was a playful smile. "You let me buy us dessert."

He grinned. "Since I know it won't be chocolate-covered bacon, I can safely say yes."

After lunch, they enjoyed the afternoon and each other's company. They checked out the different vendors and picked up a few early Christmas presents.

Jenna bought them deep-fried cookies, and they sat side by side on the bank of the lake with their decadent treats. They talked about the festival, and then the conversation turned to Jenna's family.

"I'm afraid that my biological family will trace me through the DNA test and contact me," she admitted.

"What will you do if that happens?" Cole asked.

"I'll talk it over with my parents," Jenna replied. "Depending on how they feel, I might start with exchanging some e-mails. See how things go. Make sure they're not crazy first."

He smirked. "That's probably a good idea. What about your family? Are you ready to deal with them this weekend?"

She set the half-eaten, too-rich dessert aside. "Honestly, I'm never ready to deal with Aunt Lenore. She has a tongue as sharp as a wasp, and she's twice as mean. But I'm ready to see my mom, dad, and sister. And I'm ready to talk."

"What are you going to say?" Cole asked.

Jenna couldn't believe she was having this conversation with Cole. She'd known him for such a short time, yet she was totally at ease with him. With any other guy she had dated in the past, she would have never opened up about her family situation like she had with Cole. They all would have bolted in a heartbeat.

"I'm going to tell them I understand why they didn't tell me and that the test results haven't changed anything. They're my family, and I love them." Jenna grinned. "Except now I don't have to worry that when I get older, I'll have to wear reading glasses like Dad."

He chuckled and leaned back. "I'm sure that'll make him feel better."

"Probably. If Isobel and I aren't teasing him, he gets worried," she said, then became serious. "You, your uncle, and Zoe reminded me what family was really about. You reminded me how lucky I am."

"We were only doing our civic duty." Cole plucked a small white flower that some would classify as a weed and handed it to her, but she thought it was rather sweet.

Jenna raised her brows. "Civic duty, huh?"

"Sure. I mean, what else would it be?" He grinned and bumped her shoulder with his. "It couldn't be because we like the same types of movies. Or because of your horrible basketball skills."

"Hey, I won fair and square in that game," she protested.

"I spotted you three points."

"I won by six." Jenna poked him in the chest for emphasis and laughed. "So it's just sympathy?"

"Well, you've got okay taste in ice cream. And we do agree on bacon and chocolate. And when I'm with you I feel like I'm right where I'm meant to be. Does that sound corny?"

"No, not at all," she said. "It sounds exactly how I feel."

Jenna let his words sink in and tried not to get her hopes up. After all, it hadn't even been a week. No one could fall in love that quickly. Could they?

What if Cole was the one? Would they come back to Magnolia

Harbor to get married? Of course! There would be no question that his uncle would perform the ceremony, which would take place at the Magnolia Harbor Inn in the lovely barn. She'd even talk Grace and Charlotte into letting her dress Winston up with a bow tie, and he could be their ring bearer.

Rolling her eyes at her ridiculous thoughts, Jenna jumped up and grabbed Cole's hand. "Come on. Let's go work off those cookies."

21

Charlotte

Charlotte needed her head examined.

And she needed to learn how to say no and ask for help. Neither word slipped past Charlotte's lips easily. If they had, she wouldn't have been on the run since six that morning. First, she'd had to take care of breakfast for the inn, although Grace had offered. She couldn't put all her responsibilities on her sister. Which was why when she was done with breakfast, she had stuck around to help with the housekeeping. Thankfully, both Eden and Jenna had planned to be at the festival, so there would be no hors d'oeuvres to prepare for the evening social hour.

Then Charlotte had spent the next several hours at The Tidewater working the lunch shift and prepping for the dinner crowd. Ruby had things under control and wouldn't need Charlotte's assistance for a few hours, which gave her time to check in on the baking competition at the festival.

There were two parts to the competition: the people's choice and the judge's awards. The first round of judging would be by festival attendees. Then later on they'd have the official contest with her three judges—Penny Abrams, Mimi Beale, and Roy Bevins—who were not allowed near the baking competition during the first round. That way they wouldn't have any preconceived opinions.

Charlotte checked in the next entry, a beautiful pumpkin pie with small crust stars on top and artistic dollops of whipped cream around the edges.

As the woman left, Charlotte closed her eyes to run everything she needed to do through her head. They had no idea when Dean would be back. But it was okay. They had it covered.

"Charlotte?"

Her head snapped up, and she blinked a couple of times to clear her vision. She wondered if she'd actually dozed off. Then she smiled at Jenna and Cole standing in front of her. "It's so nice to see you both. Are you having a good time?"

"We are." Jenna smiled brightly. "We've been checking out the vendor booths, and we had a great lunch and amazing deep-fried cookies."

"Oh, those cookies sound delicious. Maybe even what I need to give me a pick-me-up. I think I fell asleep sitting here." Charlotte shook her head in disbelief. How could she sleep with everything going on around her? People were talking and laughing, not to mention there was a lot of noise from the music and games.

"I'll get one for you," Cole offered. "Would you like anything else? Some sweet tea?"

"That would be great," Charlotte said. "Thank you."

The women watched him walk off.

"That was thoughtful of him," Charlotte remarked.

Jenna beamed. "I know. He's so sweet. I keep waiting to wake up and find out this was only a dream. Or for him to rear his ugly side."

"I swear he's not like that," Charlotte said. "I've known him for a while, and he really is one of the good guys."

"So why didn't you scoop him up?" Jenna asked.

It was a valid question. And it wasn't that Charlotte hadn't thought about it herself. "Honestly, there was never any zing between us. No spark of anything but friendship. I don't think there's a whole lot of great guys like him out there, and I wonder if there's one for me."

"I know the right guy for you is out there," Jenna said. "He might even be right under your nose, but you've stuck him in the friend zone and now you can't see the potential for what it is."

"You mean Dean because I'm helping him out?" Charlotte asked.

"Well, it's certainly telling that I didn't mention his name, but you did."

Charlotte stifled a sigh. She'd seen this before. Whenever one of her friends was in a new romance, it was like love endorphins flooded her system, and she was overtaken with the urge to play matchmaker. "I promise we're just friends."

"Maybe you should think about what it would be like to have more than friendship with him," Jenna said, then smiled. "Okay, I'll stop nagging now. I wanted to thank you for introducing me to Cole and let you know I'm heading home today. I've already promised Grace that I'll come back and visit again. It's only about an hour's drive."

Charlotte gave her a tight hug. "We're going to miss you. Next time I go to the city, I'll give you a call and we'll get together." She glanced up and noticed Cole returning with her food. "That is, if you have any free time."

Jenna blushed.

Cole walked up and handed Charlotte a small bag and a glass of sweet tea.

Charlotte thanked him for the snack, then told the happy couple to go enjoy their last few hours together.

Jenna and Cole waved as they walked away.

Since opening the inn, Charlotte and Grace had met a lot of interesting people from all over the country. Some became repeat customers, and the sisters loved seeing them on their return trips and catching up. A few of their guests, like Jenna and Eden, became friends, and it was hard to say goodbye.

Several more people stopped by to drop off their entries for the baking competition and to volunteer to judge. One of them was Captain Keith Daley.

"It's good to see you," Charlotte told the captain. "What can I do for you today?"

The short, fit man's dark eyes sparkled as he ran his hand over his bald head. "I believe it's my duty to test out these entries. Make sure they're all up to snuff."

"Oh, absolutely." Charlotte grinned. "To serve and protect."

"Could you, uh . . ." Daley glanced around sheepishly. "Could you not mention my participation to Helen?"

Charlotte's mouth dropped open. "You want me to lie to your wife?"

"No, no, no. Maybe don't mention it. Sort of leave the judges anonymous. That's probably for the best anyway, so whoever loses doesn't get sore and do something foolish that'll land them in my jail cell later on."

Charlotte tapped her pen against the judging sign-up sheet. Helen was a lovely woman and one of Winnie's closest friends. She couldn't outright lie to her, because that was wrong on too many levels. "Tell me why."

The captain shook his head and sighed. "She's got us on some weird new diet. I can't eat anything processed or from a box and absolutely no sugar. Now I don't mind eating healthy and all, but a man's got to have a piece of pie once in a while."

Charlotte could see both sides and couldn't help but chuckle. "I think you're right, and we should have anonymous judging. We wouldn't want anything to happen that might discourage someone from volunteering again next time." She winked and wrote down his name. "See you soon for the tasting."

"I'll be here," Daley said, then walked away.

Charlotte was still chuckling when she spotted another familiar person heading her way.

Eden walked over and greeted Charlotte.

"I'm sorry I missed you this morning," Charlotte said.

"Don't worry about it," Eden said, setting a cloth-lined basket down on the table. "I kept busy."

"How are you feeling?" Charlotte asked.

Eden beamed. "Like a new woman."

Charlotte studied Eden. There was something different about her. Charlotte noticed Eden's rosy cheeks, and she realized it wasn't only her coloring that had improved. It was the light in her eyes, the tall, strong, confident posture Charlotte hadn't seen before. This was Charlotte's first glimpse of Eden as a business executive. Yet at the same time, Eden didn't appear buttoned-up. Instead, she wore a casual cranberry sweater dress, and her hair was down, falling softly over her shoulders.

"You look fabulous," Charlotte said. "And whatever is in that basket smells equally fabulous. What have you got?"

Eden smiled. "I made heart-healthy muffins all by myself. Well, mostly. Grace and Winnie offered me some pointers. And don't worry. Grace gave me permission to use the kitchen first, and I left it spotless."

"I wasn't worried." Charlotte took the basket, and a hint of sweetness tickled her nose. She inspected the contents. The muffins were perfectly browned with no burned edges, and bits of berries peeked through. If they tasted as good as they looked, Charlotte's job was done. "As your teacher, I feel it's my obligation to test one first. I mean, my reputation is on the line."

Eden nodded, but she bit her lip, clearly holding back her laughter.

Charlotte selected a muffin and weighed it in her hand. It wasn't too heavy, but it would be filling. She easily removed the wrapper, noting the bread was moist. Tearing it in half revealed plump blueberries, chunks of strawberries, and sunflower seeds.

But the final test was the taste. Charlotte took a bite. She closed her eyes and savored the sweet and slightly salty combination. "It's delicious."

"Thank you," Eden said, smiling. "I wanted to use almonds, but I felt they needed something to make them stand out. Then I remembered one time when my grandmother put sunflower seeds on fruit salad."

"It's an excellent substitute, and I think you deserve an A." Charlotte couldn't help but stare at Eden. She seemed like a totally different woman. "Do you mind me making a personal observation?"

"Not at all."

"You've changed during your stay. It's like when you arrived you were a caterpillar—capable, steady, but missing something."

"And now?" Eden asked.

"You're the most amazing butterfly I've ever seen," Charlotte said. "You're full of grace and strength that can take on any wind and fly hundreds of miles—not that I know if butterflies do that or not. The point is, you're radiating confidence and power, and everyone's eyes are drawn to you." She grinned. "I'd like to think it's the result of my cooking lessons."

Eden chuckled. "You can definitely take some of the credit. And so can Grace, Winnie, Jenna, and The Busy Bees." She leaned in close. "I'll let you in on a little secret. I thought Magnolia Harbor would be a sleepy town with nothing to offer. But I was so wrong."

"I'm glad to hear that, but I'm sure you're eager to get home and back to work now that you're feeling better."

"Maybe," Eden said.

Charlotte wondered why Eden didn't sound more enthusiastic.

Before she could say anything else, another contestant in the baking competition arrived.

"I'll fill you in on the rest later," Eden told Charlotte. "When are the winners announced?"

"The first round of judging starts in an hour," Charlotte answered. "But we won't announce the winners until the official festival judges are done."

Eden thanked her and hurried off.

After Charlotte checked in the contestant, she set out the baking entries and got the judges ready.

By the time she finished, it felt like her head would explode. It was probably more from the lack of sleep, stress, and the constant chatter of Dolly Batten than anything else.

Dolly was the town's police dispatcher, so she knew everyone and everything going on in town. She loved to talk, and she loved to be the center of attention even more. Her long blonde hair was teased to gravity-defying heights. She wore bright-red lipstick, and her nails were pumpkin orange.

Ruby had called earlier, and business was slow for the moment at The Tidewater, which gave Charlotte a little break. Unfortunately, it also meant that she didn't have an excuse to escape from Dolly.

Grace and Spencer approached, waving.

Saved at last, Charlotte thought. She left Dolly in charge of the judges and excused herself to meet Grace and Spencer halfway. "I'm glad you both made it."

"Am I too late to sign up to judge?" Spencer asked.

"I'm afraid so," Charlotte said. "We have a lot of entries, and even still, I had to turn away judges. This town likes their baked goods."

"It's probably for the best," Spencer said. "I'm trying to eat healthier, and my doctor recommended cutting out sugar and refined carbs."

He smiled at Charlotte. "Obviously, the man has never tried one of your pies."

"Maybe Charlotte can make a special one for you with no sugar," Grace suggested.

"Can you make pecan pie without sugar?" Spencer asked.

Charlotte nodded. "And you'll never know the difference. All it takes is using the right substitute."

Grace pulled her sister aside. "Speaking of substitute, have you heard from Dean?"

Charlotte appreciated Grace's discretion. She still didn't feel comfortable sharing Dean's private matters with anyone besides her sister and aunt. "He called while I was prepping for lunch at The Tidewater."

"How's his mom doing?"

"There's no word on her post-surgery test yet," Charlotte replied. "But at least it seems she's gotten over being miffed at Dean and his brother for showing up and is enjoying their visit. Hopefully, she's taking full advantage and letting them spoil her rotten."

"How's Dean handling everything?" Concern etched deep in the lines across Grace's forehead and between her brows.

"He says he's doing okay," Charlotte said. "But I could hear the stress in his voice. He's worried about his mom and everything at home."

"That's to be expected. I'm sure he knows the restaurant is in good hands with you in charge." Grace crossed her arms, going on the defense, clearly ready to come to her sister's defense, if needed.

"Relax." Charlotte laughed. "Dean was more concerned with taking me away from the inn and leaving everything on your shoulders than he was about his business. He didn't even ask what today's specials were."

"So you were his first priority." Grace arched her brow and eyed Charlotte questioningly. "Now that is an interesting twist."

"Grace . . ." Charlotte let the warning trail off for all the good it would do.

Her sister shrugged. "I'm only making an observation. Maybe there's more going on here than what it seems. Dean doesn't usually put anything or anyone above his business."

Charlotte nudged Grace as she motioned to Spencer. "He'd be lost without your friendship, which is all that's between Dean and me too."

Grace slipped an arm around her sister's shoulder and leaned her head to rest against Charlotte's. "Are you sure that's how Dean feels too?"

Stunned, Charlotte didn't know what to say.

Grace stepped back and smiled. "It's not beyond the realm of possibilities. You two have a lot of history and a friendly rivalry about your cooking. There's chemistry. What kind of chemistry is a question only you can answer."

Charlotte remained silent.

"If you don't mind, I'm going to grab dinner," Grace said, changing the subject. "I want to get back before you announce the winners."

"That's fine," Charlotte told her. "Go ahead and get something to eat."

After Grace left, Charlotte collected the judges' scorecards. Her heart soared with pride when she saw her student's number mentioned several times. Even if Eden didn't end up winning, she had come a long way in a short time.

Sort of like Charlotte and Dean.

She let her sister's words play over in her mind. Grace was right that there was history between Charlotte and Dean and a friendly rivalry about their cooking. Both were stubborn. She wasn't too proud to admit she had flaws, but did all that point to more than just two bullheaded chefs competing to be number one?

Or could it be more?

When Charlotte had been matched with Dean on a blind date, her jaw could have hit the floor. There had been no doubt in her mind that it had been a big mistake.

But now she wondered if maybe it wasn't. Could Dean really be her perfect match? Sure, he was fun to be around, but was Jenna right? Had the right guy been under her very nose all along?

22

Jenna

As Jenna and Cole strolled around the festival, they ran into Eden.

"You look amazing in your new dress," Jenna said. "I'm so glad we caught you because I checked out of the inn early and I'm leaving soon."

"I'm sorry to hear that," Eden said. "I hope everything is okay."

"It's only a change of plans. Everything is fine," Jenna assured her. "We'll have to keep in touch."

"Definitely," Eden said with a smile. "I have some news." She told Jenna about her plans to relocate to the Charleston area.

"That's wonderful," Jenna said. "I'd be more than happy to show you around Charleston so you find the right place."

"Thank you," Eden said, giving Jenna a hug.

After they said goodbye, Jenna and Cole continued their walk. They ended up at the game booths.

"One more game?" Cole picked up a basketball and spun it around on his index finger.

Cole was good, but so was she. He might have the height on her, which would be to his advantage during a regular game, but this one was designed for those who stood five feet and under. "Are you sure you don't want me to spot you a few points this time?"

Cole chuckled as he took his place.

They played the best two out of three. She won the first, and they tied in the second and had to go into overtime—not that the kids' game really had overtime, but Zoe was manning the booth and she called it.

Cole won the second game by sheer luck. The ball hit the backboard, bounced off and hit her game's hoop, and then bounced back into his basket. After his victory, she was so thrown off that he skunked her in the third game.

But when Cole handed her a stuffed frog with a crown, Jenna didn't mind losing at all. "Are you my frog prince?"

He smiled. "Guess we'll have to wait and see."

Jenna smiled too. As she glanced around the festival, she couldn't believe how much time had passed. She hadn't intended to stay this long, but she'd been having such a great time with Cole.

The sun had started to sink beyond the horizon, painting the sky a myriad of colors as hundreds of fairy lights began to twinkle throughout the waterfront park. It was like a warning that it was time for her to leave. As it was, she was going to hit rush hour in Charleston. But instead of heading toward the parking area, she silently bargained for one more minute.

At that moment, music from the other end of the park started, and she could hear Pastor Abrams inviting everyone over to the dance floor. The dance that Cole had invited her to was starting, and she wasn't even wearing her new dress. It was packed inside her suitcase in her car.

"I'm sorry, but I should go," Jenna said. "Mom starts baking at five in the morning, which means I need to be up by four."

"You could bring your family to the festival tomorrow," Cole suggested. "They could enjoy the dog show, the kids' talent show, and all the other stuff going on."

Jenna laughed. "I'm not about to subject you to Aunt Lenore. Besides, it's this whole tradition. Cooking all day. Dad watches TV. Board games. The cousins come over and talk and argue. It gets loud and obnoxious. I don't want to scare you off."

"It'll take more than a mean aunt and a crazy family to chase me away."

"What about an overprotective big sister?" she asked.

"Doesn't scare me."

Jenna stopped walking. She bit her lip and stared at Cole. He was too good to be true. The majority of guys she'd dated didn't ask to meet her family or want to listen to her spill her guts or talk about her feelings. They kept things light and casual. Cole was like her very own fairy-tale prince come to life.

"Stop thinking so much," Cole said. "Is it so hard to believe that I'm exactly what you see?"

"How did you know—"

"It's written all over your face," he said, interrupting her. "Look, I like you. You're funny and smart, good with animals and kids, and you're kind and giving. You make me laugh, and I can talk to you about anything. I'd say that's worth exploring. But first what I'd really like is one dance with you before you have to leave. Say yes?"

Jenna smiled. "Yes."

Cole led her to the dance floor and pulled her close. "I'm glad we were able to come to the dance together after all."

"Me too." As they danced, Jenna marveled yet again at how fortunate she was to have met Cole.

The song ended too soon. Cole walked Jenna to her car to make sure she was safe—as if it were possible to be unsafe in Magnolia Harbor. "Can I take you to lunch on Monday?"

"I'd love that," she said.

"How about dinner and the movies on Friday too?" Cole asked. "I thought about picking Tuesday or Wednesday, but I don't want to sound pushy."

Jenna laughed. "Friday works for me."

"Until Monday then." Cole brushed his lips over Jenna's in a sweet kiss and smiled. "See, not a frog."

Jenna was disappointed to leave, but her heart was feeling much lighter. She'd finally come to terms with her past and was ready to face her family and her future.

23

Eden

The heart attack had given Eden a fresh start, a second chance at life, a do-over to get it right, and she had every intention of succeeding this time around.

Calling Randall Bergman, her boss, and resigning had been harder than signing her divorce papers, which said something about her marriage all those years ago. Her stomach had tossed and turned. Black spots had danced before her eyes. She'd almost chickened out.

Before she could get the words out, Randall had asked, "Are you going to at least come back and clean out your office, or should I do it for you?"

Randall admitted that he'd known for months that her mind wasn't fully on her job anymore, and he was sorry it had taken something as drastic as standing at death's door to get her attention. He'd miss her, but he understood her decision and fully supported it. In fact, he'd even promised to send some business her way.

She'd recommended Fred for her job and gave her resignation. That was step one.

Step two had been to talk to Addie and Louise from the Serenity Boutique. When Eden had explained her plan to them, they were fully on board and happy to not only help but to keep working with Eden.

Step three had been making plans with Jenna. In the last week, Eden had fallen in love with Magnolia Harbor and South Carolina, so much so that she planned to relocate. Jenna had agreed to show her around Charleston so Eden could find the right place to settle in for her new life.

With all the pieces in place, Eden couldn't wait to share her news with Charlotte, Grace, Winnie, and the other Busy Bees.

Eden spotted Grace and Spencer standing next to Winnie in the crowd surrounding a table filled with baked goods. Charlotte was conferring with the judges.

"Did I miss the big announcement?" Eden asked as she joined them.

"You're just in time," Winnie said to Eden. "They're going to announce the winners any minute."

"I'm pulling for each of you." Grace held up her hands to show fingers crossed on both hands.

"You can always have a do-over back at the inn, and I'll be the judge," Spencer offered.

"You'd declare it a tie." Grace poked Spencer playfully on the shoulder, laughing. "Besides, I thought you were trying to eat healthier."

He held his hands up in surrender with a smile. "Can't blame a guy for doing the neighborly thing."

Eden didn't know where she'd land, but she hoped she'd find friends as great as the ones she'd found here in Magnolia Harbor.

A hush fell over the crowd as Charlotte climbed the stairs to the podium.

"Thank you everyone for attending our first Holidaze Festival," Charlotte began. "And thanks to everyone who entered the baking competition and offered to judge. We had a bigger response than we expected. When Pastor Abrams wants to raise money for the food pantry again, he should hold more bake sales because the desserts have been a huge hit."

The crowd laughed.

"For our first round, the People's Choice, the winner is . . ." Charlotte paused for dramatic effect. "Phyllis Gendel, our head librarian, with her amazing mint chocolate icebox pie."

Upon hearing that the winning entry was a pie, Eden's first thought was that she shouldn't have chosen something healthy to enter in the contest. Then she chided herself for being a sore loser. It didn't matter if she won or lost. She was a new person now.

Eden joined the others in clapping as a woman with short gray hair took the podium. She had high cheekbones, a pronounced chin, and blue eyes that sparked with authority. Eden would bet that when Phyllis was on duty the library was completely quiet.

"An icebox pie, as you all know, is a classic Southern dessert, which is why I picked this recipe," Phyllis said. "What some of you may not know is the icebox dates back to . . ."

When Phyllis wrapped up her talk, the crowd gave her a rousing round of applause.

Winnie smiled at Eden. "I might have to make an icebox pie next time."

"I'd be happy to be your test subject," Spencer said.

"Have you always had such a sweet tooth?" Grace teased. She shook her head, looking the man up and down like she was trying to figure out where he put all those calories.

Eden couldn't blame her because he did seem like the type who lived on lean protein and ran ten miles a day.

"It's from my time working for the FBI," Spencer replied. "Long days, erratic hours, grabbing what I could eat on the run. Most of the time that was fast food, muffins, or a candy bar to give me a shot of energy. Old habits are hard to break, but I'm trying to do better."

Eden liked that. Maybe that should be her new motto. *Old habits are hard to break, but I'm trying to do better.*

Needlepoint could be her next project, and then she could hang the saying on the wall facing her desk as a daily reminder. Or she could dial it back and simply print it out, instead of being crafty. She needed to remember that moderation was her friend.

"Well, now that we know, we can help," Grace said.

"Starting by not making you an icebox pie," Winnie finished with a smile.

Spencer groaned good-naturedly.

The group laughed.

Charlotte retook the podium. "Before I announce the official judges' results, I'd like to mention the prizes. First place is a food processor, second is a six-piece essential bakeware set, and third is a colorful set of nesting prep bowls." She smiled. "Our winners will go home with everything they need to bake up more scrumptious goodies for us."

The crowd gave another round of applause, along with some cheering and a few requests for desserts.

Charlotte wasn't joking about the town's love of desserts. Not that Eden could blame them, as she was right there with them all.

"Okay, now for the official judges' results. Is everyone ready?" Charlotte waited for the crowd to respond. "In third place, we have Tammy Snyder for her banana bread."

The audience clapped.

"Second place goes to Eden Masterson with her nutty fruit muffins," Charlotte said.

"What did she say?" Eden asked in shock.

"You got second place," Spencer answered.

"Congratulations," Grace said to Eden. "That's fabulous."

"Oh, I knew those muffins were a winner," Winnie commented with a smile. "Well done."

"And first place is awarded to Winnie Bennett for her pumpkin pie," Charlotte announced.

The crowd applauded and cheered.

Eden, Grace, and Spencer congratulated Winnie.

Still stunned, Eden said, "Did I really get second?"

"There's nothing wrong with second," Winnie said, obviously trying to console her. "Personally, I think your muffins were much better than my pie. If it wasn't so close to Thanksgiving, they would have won. But people like their comfort foods, and you can't beat pumpkin pie in November. I should have made something else. It was like cheating."

"You've never cheated at anything in your life," Grace told her aunt.

Eden smiled and took both women's hands. "Second place is wonderful. It's certainly more than I ever expected, and it wouldn't have happened without the two of you. Thank you so much."

Eden meant every word too. In her previous life before the heart attack, she never would have settled for anything less than first place. If she hadn't won, she would have analyzed what had gone wrong, strategized how to fix it, and tried again and again until she'd taken home the blue ribbon. Or in this case, the food processor. Life had been all about the prize, not the journey. Actually, she'd been so focused on the flag at the end of the race that she hadn't paid attention to the scenery along the way.

But her time in Magnolia Harbor had taught her that she'd missed out on so much. Life wasn't about winning. That wasn't what brought true happiness. The journey was what brought the joy in life.

Earlier that day as she'd made her muffins, Grace and Winnie had kept her company in the kitchen. They'd talked about loss, love, and life and shared stories of their first crushes, heartbreaks, and embarrassing moments.

Eden had confessed to the time she'd accidentally jumped into the wrong car and almost kissed the wrong man behind the wheel. In her defense, she had been in a hurry, it was raining, and she had water in her eyes. Oh, how they'd laughed.

She wouldn't trade one second of that for a blue ribbon or a food processor.

Charlotte joined the group, grinning from ear to ear. "You guys rocked the competition. The judges loved your entries."

"I'm so glad," Eden said.

"I hope you don't mind," Charlotte said to Eden, "but Penny Abrams asked if she could take the rest of your muffins with her. She's the pastor's wife and wanted to share them with her husband."

"Not at all," Eden said. "I'm flattered. But I'm trying to figure out what I'm going to do with all that bakeware."

"I don't think you'll have a problem putting it to good use," Charlotte said. "It's all boxed up, so it'll make the drive home without getting broken."

"About my trip home—" Before Eden could break the news that she was planning to move, her phone rang. It was Fred. She wondered what her former assistant wanted now. "Please excuse me a minute. I need to take this."

The others nodded.

Eden stepped away. "I'm surprised to hear from you."

"I can't believe you quit," Fred said, a note of panic in his voice. "We have another huge problem, and I don't know what to do. I can't handle it on my own."

"You've got this," Eden assured him. "You've more than got this, and if I didn't believe that, I wouldn't have told Randall that you should be promoted to fill my job. Now, pull it together and solve the problem."

Before Fred could protest, Eden hung up. She turned around to find everyone staring at her in shock. "I quit my job this afternoon."

"What?" Charlotte asked.

"Good for you," Grace said.

Winnie put a hand over her heart. "Oh my."

"It sounds like congratulations are in order," Spencer said.

Every time Eden acknowledged what she'd done, a wave of shock washed over her, with her stomach completing a series of flips and flops worthy of a ten on any Olympic scale. She gave herself a moment to settle down before responding. "Thank you. I'm pretty excited. To be honest, I couldn't have done it without all of you."

"What will you do now?" Winnie asked.

"I'm starting my own consulting firm for small businesses," Eden replied. "I'll be assisting them with public relations issues, such as how to gain exposure and get their names out in their community without breaking their budgets. And I already have my first client. The Serenity Boutique."

"Those are the ladies who came to the inn, right?" Grace asked.

Eden nodded. "I'm also going to be relocating. Jenna has offered to show me around the Charleston area so I can find a place to live. Atlanta has been good to me, but it's time for a fresh start, and I can't think of anywhere else I'd rather be."

"We should have a celebration," Charlotte said. "But I need to get over to The Tidewater. How about a special breakfast tomorrow morning?"

Everyone agreed.

Charlotte told Eden how proud she was of her before taking off. Then Winnie excused herself to go find her husband, Gus.

Spencer motioned to the area where the dance was being held. "I was thinking about going over there to listen to the music. Would you ladies care to join me?"

"That sounds nice," Grace said.

"I'm going to claim my prize and take it to the car," Eden said. "I'll see you over there in a little while."

"Congratulations again," Grace said, then waved as she and Spencer walked away.

After storing her new bakeware in the car, Eden wandered around the festival with no particular goal in mind. For the moment, she had no task, no items on a to-do list, nothing to worry about. She'd made a decision and had executed the plan. For the first time in a long time, she really was on vacation, and she had no clue what to do. It was like arriving in Magnolia Harbor all over again.

Except instead of cynicism, she now had a clear vision of the future.

Eden let her feet lead the way, stopping every now and then to say hello to people she'd met over the past week.

She ended up on the outskirts of the dance area, where she found a spot to observe. The band was playing a lively two-step. Even from a distance, Eden could see the twinkle in Winnie's eyes as Gus twirled her around, making her laugh like a schoolgirl.

Spencer and Grace were also on the dance floor. They made a beautiful couple, and Eden wondered if the two of them would ever acknowledge the chemistry between them. She sure hoped so, because it was obvious they were interested in each other.

Judith from The Busy Bees called to Eden, then sat down beside her. "Good to see you here. Are you enjoying the music?"

"I am. Is your husband playing?"

Judith nodded. "There he is. The tall, bald guy playing the guitar like he's the king of rock. Ken will be sore after tonight, but he'll have a smile on his face for the next week."

"Happy spouse, happy life," Eden joked.

"You know it." Judith nudged Eden's shoulder. "Are you going to dance? I could introduce you to some good-looking single men."

"No." She sighed, as there was nothing she'd love more. "The doctor told me to take it easy. I'm not sure the two-step is what he had in mind."

"Not all of those songs require the two-step," Judith argued.

"Some of them are nice and slow. Perfect for taking it easy and getting to know someone new."

Eden laughed. The woman wasn't exactly subtle. "Did you have someone in mind?"

"Well, now that you ask. Ken's cousin from Charleston is visiting. Sweet man. Lost his wife a couple of years ago. It would be wonderful if he had someone to dance with."

How was Eden supposed to say no after a comment like that? Besides, she'd been dreaming of dancing all week long. And she'd bought a new dress. It would be a shame to let it go to waste. One dance couldn't hurt, right? It had been so long since she'd stepped onto the dance floor that she didn't know if she even remembered how to keep the rhythm.

But sitting on the sidelines had never been for her and she refused to let life pass her by, so when Judith nudged her again and flashed her a smile, Eden laughed. "Just one dance."

24

Charlotte

There were hundreds of people milling around the waterfront the following afternoon, but Charlotte had never felt so alone. It was a strange feeling in a town where she knew most everyone, and apparently they were all here. She couldn't go more than two feet without someone stopping her to chat.

She tried to cheer herself up by recalling the pastor's announcement that morning. They'd already raised enough money to keep the food pantry going for the next six months. It was more than any of them had hoped for when they'd first planned the event.

It was a day for celebrations, yet the one person she wanted to share the success with the most wasn't here, which in itself boggled her mind. Maybe it was a good thing Dean was still out of town. Apparently she needed the time away from him to get her head straight. Out of sight, out of mind, right? Unfortunately, she seemed to be subscribing to the theory of absence making the heart grow fonder instead.

Charlotte took a deep breath, weaving through the crowd toward the stage. Surely once Dean was home and back to his usual self, she would remember how he could make her teeth grind and set her nerves on edge, how he liked to argue that his way was always the best, and that he had to have the last word. She'd forget all about the vulnerable side of him, the soft side, the side that laughed easily at her jokes and trusted her with his kitchen.

Dean had a bit of an ego, but he was a great guy. He loved kids—even coached Little League and volunteered with several of the fund-raisers that benefited the children's wing of the local hospital. He cared about his staff and friends and the community. On many levels, he was exactly what Charlotte was searching for. The matchmaking service had thought they were perfect for each other too.

But she wasn't convinced.

For now, she promised the pastor she'd check in with Cole to see if he needed any help with the talent show. Wrangling twenty kids ages three to thirteen was way out of the guy's league, but he'd stepped up like a trouper when they needed the assistance. It wasn't Charlotte's area of expertise either, but she still hadn't learned how to say no.

"Charlotte, wait up."

She whipped around at the sound of Dean's voice. An unstoppable smile spread over her face, and she forgot her worries over failed magic tricks, wayward hula hoops, or some kid breaking a bone instead of a board with his karate chop.

Dean looked good. Charlotte took in the natural smile that lit up his eyes, sans the dark circles he'd sported a few days ago. And he wore a cashmere sweater and nice jeans. No, *good* wasn't the right word. *Relaxed* and *happy* fit Dean better.

Okay, she couldn't deny it was great to see her friend again. It didn't mean anything more than that. At least that was what she told herself at the moment.

"I didn't know you were going to be home today," Charlotte said. "Why didn't you tell me?"

"Sorry. I thought you'd be happier to see me. I can leave."

"No." She laughed at his playful offer. "You're right on time for the talent show. It's all yours. But how's your mom?"

His smile grew three times as large. "She's fine. She doesn't have cancer."

"That's wonderful news." Charlotte threw herself into his arms, laughing and crying at the same time. She held on, overcome with relief, joy, and an awareness of how good it felt to have Dean's arms wrapped around her.

Suddenly conscious that the hug had lasted too long, Charlotte stepped back, running her hands over her hair to fix her ponytail. "I was thinking that today was a day to celebrate, and that's the best news ever."

"Her doctors are still a little unsure what is going on with her cells," he said. "But they know it's not cancer and it's nothing worrisome, as they put it. So after a big celebration dinner, my mom kicked me and Marc out."

"Your mom kicked you out?" She grinned. "I really do like her."

"Very funny." Dean stepped closer to let a few people pass, then ushered her over to an empty picnic table, where they could speak in private.

She hadn't even noticed the basket he'd been carrying until he set it down on the table.

"She wanted us to get back to our lives," Dean went on. "Marc to his wife and kids and me to the restaurant. So she gave us an hour to pack and sent us on our way." He laughed. "That woman is a force to be reckoned with."

"She sounds like it. And is your dad okay now too?"

"Yeah." Dean dropped his head, arms resting on his knees. "He broke down and cried when the call came. I've never seen him cry before."

"It had to be such a relief to him. To all of you." Charlotte took his hand and squeezed it. She had to make contact, to let him know she understood. The crisis was over, but she knew that stress was still pumping through Dean, the what-ifs running through his mind that wouldn't go away with one phone call.

"It was, but this situation has made me realize that I need to slow down and take more time to enjoy life. The restaurant is doing well.

I have to trust Ruby and let her take on more responsibilities." Dean glanced at her, as if trying to gauge her reaction to his words, to see if they were on the same page.

Unsure if he was feeling her out about them or Ruby, Charlotte took the easy road. "She's ready."

"Good." Dean broke eye contact for a moment as if he were regrouping, then gave Charlotte a smile so soft it was barely there. "I wanted to thank you for all your help. I don't know what I would have done without you. You were my anchor when I was losing it."

"It was nothing." She turned away so he couldn't see the blush stealing over her cheeks or the shimmer of tears in her eyes.

Dean caught her hand. "It was everything and more. You let me vent, counseled me, and ran my kitchen. You kept me going and gave me hope when I had none left."

Charlotte swiped at the tears that escaped, embarrassed by her sentimental reaction to his words, not even sure why they affected her so much. "You'd have done the same for me."

Dean handed her the basket of goodies, grinning. "It's not enough, but thank you."

Determined to lighten the mood, she pushed away her churning emotions to be examined at another time. Today was a day for celebrations, not tears.

"Is there chocolate?" Charlotte asked. "Because chocolate's always a good start."

Together they laughed as she explored the basket's contents. He'd gone all out with gourmet spices, a cute kitchen apron, and a stuffed chef bear. And of course, gourmet chocolate. There was hope for Dean yet.

Charlotte picked up the bear. "Does he have a name?"

"I thought I'd let you choose it," Dean answered.

"I'll have to give it some thought." She pretended to mull it over. "Maybe Chef Green Goo after your hollandaise masterpiece."

Dean laughed.

His deep laughter lifted her mood and made her feel like a giddy teen. She liked him this way, easygoing, happy, and not trying to prove himself. Was this the real Dean Bradley or a temporary side effect from the stress of dealing with his mom's health scare? Once he settled back into his old routine, would he start annoying her again with his ego? She truly hoped not.

"Maybe we could get together for coffee sometime," Dean said. "We could exchange cooking tips or even recipes. Or not talk cooking at all. We could talk sports or movies or gardening."

"You garden?" Charlotte asked. Somehow she couldn't see Dean down on his knees, getting his pants dirty.

"The Tidewater does have a garden, but I don't take care of it." He picked up her bear and pretended like the stuffed animal was asking. "What do you say, coffee to start with?"

Charlotte smiled. "Maybe." After all, she couldn't make it too easy for him.

Dean stood and began to back away toward the stage, giving her a heart-melting grin. "I can work with maybe."

As she watched Dean leave, Grace and Winnie joined her. They peeked at the contents of the basket, then followed Charlotte's gaze.

"It seems the two of you have turned a corner in your friendship." Grace smiled innocently as she picked up the bear.

"It's just a thank-you gift," Charlotte insisted.

"It's a rather extravagant gift," Grace remarked. "Didn't you once tell me that saffron is the most expensive spice there is? Followed by vanilla, cardamom, cloves, and cinnamon? And I don't know much about cooking, but these look like high-quality versions. Also, a stuffed animal. Guys don't give stuffed animals to women they only consider friends." She turned to Winnie. "Wouldn't you agree?"

"I do believe you're on to something," Winnie answered. "Maybe I should ask Mr. Bradley what his intentions are with our Charlotte."

Charlotte gasped in horror. "You'll do no such thing!"

Grace and Winnie burst into laughter.

Charlotte rolled her eyes. "You two are incorrigible." Then she laughed, knowing they were teasing. Winnie would never ask Dean his intentions. She might play matchmaker, but she wouldn't interfere on that level.

When their laughter died down, Charlotte changed the subject. "Did Eden get checked out okay? I'm going to miss her and Jenna. They definitely didn't feel like guests at the inn."

"Yes, and Eden said she'd call as soon as she found her new place," Grace said. "But I know what you mean. We've met so many wonderful people since we opened our doors, but those two were special."

"Have you heard anything else from Jenna?" Charlotte asked.

"I let her know that Winston took home the blue ribbon and there'd be no living with him now," Grace answered. "She was thrilled that he did so well. Also, she said her reunion with her family was going well. She'll tell us all about it next week after church." She grinned. "Hopefully over your scones."

"That sounds promising for her and Cole," Winnie murmured dreamily.

"And that reminds me," Grace said to Winnie. "Jenna asked me to thank you for the Magic 8-Ball. She said its advice was spot-on all week long. It even led her to her date with Cole."

"Guess I still have the touch," Winnie said.

"We've never questioned that," Charlotte replied.

"As much as I'd like to stay and enjoy the festival," Grace said, checking her watch, "I think we'd better get back to the inn to prepare for our new guests."

"It's always exciting to meet new people," Winnie remarked. "Who's coming?"

"We've got a couple on their honeymoon, a family in for the holidays, and a retired couple traveling around the country," Grace said. "I want to make sure everything is perfect for them."

"Everything will be perfect," Charlotte assured her. "It always is, because we make a great team."

"She's right. Your parents would be so proud of what you've done, of all that you've accomplished, both on your own and together." Winnie hugged them. "I'm proud of you too and so thankful for the family I have. Now, I'm going to go see what kind of trouble Gus is up to."

Charlotte and Grace laughed and linked arms as they walked toward the parking area.

"Winnie isn't the only one who's thankful for the family she has," Grace said. "So am I. We are definitely blessed."

Charlotte thought of her wonderful, supportive family and how much she enjoyed running the Magnolia Harbor Inn with her sister. She also thought of Dean and their friendship . . . and the potential for something more.

She smiled. "Yes, we are. So very blessed."